WITCHY AWAKENING

A PARANORMAL COZY MYSTERY

MIDLIFE POTIONS
BOOK ONE

C. A. PHIPPS

Witchy Awakening is a work of fiction. Names, places, and incidents either are products of the author's imagination or are used fictitiously.

Witchy Awakening Copyright © 2023 by C. A. Phipps

All rights reserved.

No part of this book may be reproduced in any form or by any electronic or mechanical means, including information storage and retrieval systems, without written permission from the author, except for the use of brief quotations in a book review.

Cover Copyright © 2022 by Melody Simmons

bookcoversbymelody.com

For my husband.
My sounding board and first BETA reader. 🩶

WITCHY AWAKENING

Discovering you're a witch when your cat starts talking to you isn't as fun as it sounds.

After the sudden death of her mother, Jessica Lavender's mediocre life as a baker takes an unexpected turn.

Forced to return to her home town to run her mom's store, she must learn to harness her magical abilities while dealing with nosy neighbors.

If that wasn't enough, her snarky familiar insists she unearth and solve the suspicious death of the body in her garden!

This paranormal cozy mystery will have you questioning everything you thought you knew about magic and murder!

Midlife Potions
Witchy Awakening

Witchy Hot Spells
Witchy Flash Back
Witchy Bad Blood - coming soon!

Join my mailing list to find out about new releases and deals on my books.

CHAPTER
ONE

The death of Lissa Lavender shocked the small town of Good Fortune.

Lissa had been the heart and soul of the community, which meant her daughter's return to town after many years was big news.

Knowing how the small town operated, Jessica Lavender should have expected it, but the shock of being in the limelight sent her into defensive mode. That made it doubly difficult to come to grips with what the loss of her mother truly meant to her.

Arriving at night with a suitcase and her cat Maestro, she went straight to her mother's house at the end of Main Street. An hour later, the phone rang and didn't stop. Eventually she'd pulled out the connection, hoping the townsfolk would get the message.

As soon as she opened her eyes this morning, Jess knew she'd only been fooling herself. After the first thundering knock from well-meaning neighbor #1 forced Jess out of bed, she managed a quick wash, slipped into yesterday's clothes, and opened the door to an incessant flood of visitors.

Visits overlapped, and these people who were mostly strangers stayed far longer than it took to drop off a dish of recently cooked food and pay their respects.

Eventually every counter-top and table was filled with plastic containers and plates. Jess had no words left to thank them or answer their myriad questions. How she was, or what she had been up to since they'd last seen her, didn't matter right now. They didn't know her, and she didn't want to know them.

You're tired. You should tell them to leave.

The words swirled in her head, and Jess suddenly yawned in the next-door-neighbor's face—the one who had set today off into this nightmare. Jess put a hand to her mouth. "I'm so sorry, Mrs. Crandle."

The short, round woman, reminiscent of a fairy godmother, tutted. "You poor dear." She clapped her hands, and the noise in the living room and kitchen subsided. "We've outstayed our welcome, ladies. Jessica is exhausted after her journey and needs to rest."

With a few hugs and more sympathetic words, the rooms emptied as if by magic.

Jess smiled genuinely for the first time today. "Thank you, Mrs. Crandle."

"You're welcome, dear. I'll be off too, as soon as I've cleared the rest of this food into the freezer, but might I give you a few words of advice?"

Jess's smile froze, sensing that she had no real choice in the matter. "Of course, Mrs. Crandle."

The woman counted off the fingers on her left hand. "Don't touch Rebecca's stew—you'll have heartburn for days. I'd be wary of that pie from Daphne Dennison. Reg

Doherty, the local chicken farmer, told me she's been out collecting road kill again. Make sure you return all the containers if you don't want to make enemies. Get down to your mother's shop tomorrow and throw out all the expired ingredients before they rot." She was down to her last finger. "And now that you're all grown up, please call me Amy."

Jess brushed her auburn hair over one shoulder and smothered a groan. To be fair, the list seemed doable and potentially lifesaving, but she hated being told what to do. "Thank you, I'll be sure to do that."

"Don't you worry about a thing," Amy said firmly. "Your mom was always saying how capable you are, and she has plenty of friends who are only too happy to help with the arrangements."

The bit about her being capable was a surprise. Their mother-daughter relationship had been tense for more years than Jess cared to remember. When the expectations to follow in Lissa's footsteps proved too much to deal with twenty years ago, Jess moved north. If she was honest, she'd checked out on their relationship long before that. As for a team of Amy's coming back to boss her about...

"I'm sure I can manage, but please tell them I said thank you."

Amy tilted her head and after a second or two nodded before gathering up more containers. "Well, you just say the word if you change your mind."

Forcing as much as possible into the freezer and fridge, Jess finally locked the door behind Amy, and with her back pressed against it she let out a long breath.

"Now what do I do?" she muttered. It was a small house. Some might say quaint, but Jess had always considered it cramped. Clean and tidy with two bedrooms, a bathroom upstairs, and a utility room with a toilet by the back door, she hoped it would be easy to sell so she could go home.

Maestro appeared from behind the couch and sauntered across the room.

"I wondered where you'd gone to, buddy."

"If you thought I was going to put up with them patting me or clutching me to their bosoms all day, you were sorely mistaken."

Jess gaped. "You did not just talk to me."

He sat down in front of her and tilted his head exactly the way he usually did whenever she spoke to him. "See anyone else here?"

Only, he'd never answered her before. She slithered down the door and landed with a thump on her butt. "It was inevitable. I'm going crazy."

Lazily, he licked one sleek paw. "No, you're not."

She put both hands to her face and rocked. "I haven't got time for a nervous breakdown. There's too much to do."

"Then don't have one. They're overrated from what I've seen."

She peered between her fingers. "I've owned you for five years. Why would you suddenly be able to talk now? No, this is just a figment of my imagination," she added.

He stuck the paw out to her. "We'll leave the whole 'who owns who' thing aside for now. Consider this. The issue isn't about me not talking but rather that you haven't been listening."

"That doesn't make sense."

He sighed and came a little closer. "Look me in the eye and tell me you haven't heard voices in your head."

"What? Well, everyone does. That doesn't make them real."

"And you're sure about that?"

"Of course."

"Hmm. I thought you'd be quicker than this."

"What do you mean?"

"Usually when the Lavender women find out they're witches they readily grasp the concept because they've had an inkling since they were small. Then again, you've always been the most stubborn child."

Her jaw was a little sore from hanging open, and she snapped it shut for a moment at his disdain. "You're making no sense. How would you know anything about my ancestors? Or my childhood for that matter."

He sighed again, lay down, and put his face between his front paws. "Let's start from the beginning then. All Lavender women are witches. They have been since the beginning of time."

"That's just silly. My mom wasn't a witch," she interrupted.

"Is the idea of it sillier than talking to her cat?"

Jess shook her head, not sure why she was arguing with an animal who wasn't supposed to be capable of arguing back. "You're not mom's cat—you're mine."

He raised what looked like an eyebrow. "Where did I come from?"

"Is that a trick question? Mom gave you to me for my fortieth birthday," Jess told him smugly.

"Correct. Although, let me reiterate, owning me is still up for debate. Anyway, what is my lineage?"

She smirked at what was clearly a trick question. "You are mom's cat's kitten."

He sniffed rudely. "I'm a boy and have never sired any kittens—that I know of."

"That's not what I meant. Mom always had a cat. She must have had a female cat that had a kitten."

"Incorrect. That statement tells me how little you notice about your surroundings. Still, I'm not surprised after watching you for most of your life. I became her cat after her mother passed me along when she turned forty. I might add it's incredibly frustrating to train each Lavender, and I do hope we can get through your induction quicker than how it's shaping up."

Clearly he was talking rubbish. She laughed a little hysterically. Or she was hallucinating rubbish. Maybe one of the women put something dodgy in their baking. Yes, that had to be it.

"I wouldn't go around accusing people of drugging you."

Jess held her head. Cats couldn't read minds.

"Familiars can always read the minds of their witches. Unless a witch chooses to shut them out."

She gulped and peered through her fingers. He was still there, watching her with an imperious glint in his eyes. "How old are you?"

"Too old to count the years. Now, any more questions or do you need more time to think up ways to describe me?"

She stared blankly for several seconds. Even if all this nonsense was true, what did one ask a talking cat about being a witch? She stood and cautiously circled Maestro. "I'm going to bed."

He waved her away dismissively. "Sweet dreams, witch."

Jess hurried down the hall and up the stairs. A talking, snarky cat. She must be more stressed than she thought.

CHAPTER TWO

Sunlight peeked under the bottom of the curtain. Jess rolled over in the small bed and whacked her elbow on the wall. She opened one eye, winced at the bright poppy-covered wallpaper, and closed it again. It hadn't felt right to sleep in her mother's bed, but she hadn't slept on a twin mattress since she left home. Had it always been this uncomfortable? Maybe she'd have to rethink her choice of bedroom if she had to stay longer.

How long would it take to do all the necessary paperwork? She should have googled it. More than a couple of days would be too long.

"You should plan on a week minimum."

Jess peered over the side of the bed where Maestro sat staring up at her.

"I'm hungry," he said.

"So, it wasn't a dream come nightmare? You really can talk."

A paw touched his chest. "Oh dear, are we all the way back to denial?"

"If you're so clever, why don't you get your own breakfast?"

He waved both front paws under her nose. "No opposable thumbs, dummy."

"Are you always this rude?"

"I was about to say the same to you. But then I remembered that you've always been snarky."

"That is an outright lie, and you know it. You're only copying what I said or thought last night about you.

"Ah, I did recall hearing those words somewhere. Still, if the judgment fits..."

"Are you mocking me?"

"I wouldn't dare. Now hurry up." He sauntered to the door then stopped to peer over his shoulder. "You may want to smarten up some. You look terrible, and three days in the same clothes is pushing things a little far, don't you agree?"

Jess threw the covers back and crossed to the small dresser with an attached mirror. He was right. She looked like she hadn't slept in days, and her wrinkles had teamed up to play snakes and ladders on her face.

Why hadn't she been blessed with her mother's genes? Lissa Lavender barely had a laughter line, and she was twenty years older than Jess. Another thing that sucked about their relationship. Lissa had always told her that the creams she used weren't worth the bottle they came in, but Jess refused to use the stuff her mother made and sold in her shop. Naturally she'd been curious but wouldn't admit it. And now it was too late.

"I told you—stubborn." Came his voice from down the hall.

"Stop listening to my thoughts!"

She snatched some clean clothes from her opened bag

and went across the hall to the bathroom, slamming the door behind her. Her dreams had been full of the cat who owned her and resembled the Queen from Alice in Wonderland. His confidence was next level, and she didn't think she could handle another day with the Jekyll and Hyde familiar.

Jess stayed under the running water for a very long time before she could summon the will to wash herself with the bottles set on the shelf. She'd brought her own toiletries but left them in the case and was darned if she'd go back to the room to get them. The first body wash she picked up smelled like her mother, and she put that firmly back on the shelf. The second one had a smell that reminded her of the climbing rose that adorned the front fence. It was pretty and always made her smile when it was in bloom.

Grabbing a cloth from the bathroom cupboard, she scrubbed hard until she felt more alive. With a towel wrapped around her, she moisturized her face. Was her skin a little brighter today? And her hazel eyes seemed greener. Jess shrugged. It must be that something she'd eaten was affecting her eyesight as well as her imagination.

Once dried and dressed, she made her way to the kitchen where Maestro waited at his twin bowls that she'd brought with her.

"Feel better?" he asked.

"I do," she admitted despite wanting to ignore him.

"Good. Once we've eaten we should discuss your talents."

"Talents?"

He batted the bowl across the floor toward her. "Food first."

Annoyed at the demanding tone, she filled one side

with water then opened a can of cat food and placed the joined dishes on the floor by the back door.

"We also need to discuss my dietary preferences, which is the only good part of the training," he muttered before turning his back on her to delicately lap at the food.

That one act was reassuringly familiar.

Jess opened the fridge and shook her head at the stacked shelves. It should be fantastic that she didn't have to shop for food. But seriously, if she could get the whole road-kill business out of her mind and decide on what to eat three times a day, she wouldn't make a dent in this even if she stayed a week. Eventually, she took out a bottle of milk and a half-eaten apple pie. Stabbing the fork into it, she stared out to the back garden.

Weeds grew among the plants. A lot of weeds. Her mother would not have stood for it."

"She couldn't weed once she got sick."

Jess swung around, and apple pie slid from her fork to land on the floor. "Why didn't she call me, Maestro?" Embarrassed by the plaintiveness in her voice, she grabbed a napkin and wiped up the mess.

He stopped licking a paw, letting it hang in mid-air. "She did phone you several times in that last week. Lissa couldn't bring herself to mention it and upset you. Would you have come home if you knew?"

"Of course I would, if she needed me."

"If?" He scoffed. "Let's be honest. You wouldn't have believed she did."

Jess swallowed hard. "Maybe not."

Maestro lifted his shoulders. "Don't beat yourself up about it. The truth is that she hated to impose on you and wouldn't have explained the situation no matter how many times the two of you conversed."

Conversed was an interesting way to describe their conversations, and now that she thought about it she decided it was the perfect word. Plain and without emotion. Except for annoyance. They poked each other like a bear with a stick every chance they had. "If you know so much, how come you didn't tell me about the situation earlier?"

"You weren't ready to hear."

"How do you know that?"

"You don't get your powers until you're ready. I never saw an inkling of anything until a week ago."

"And when was I supposed to be ready for the bombshell?

"Menopause."

Jess blushed. "I beg your pardon?"

"Every witch is slightly different, because it's not an exact science, but the women in your family start between forty and forty-five years old. By fifty their special powers are fully developed."

"I'm a little young for that midlife stuff, but assuming that this is all true," she scoffed, "what are my powers, and how come I know nothing about any of this?"

"Like I said. You weren't ready—a late bloomer of sorts. As for your talents? You can make potions and lotions to help—or harm."

"Potions and lotions!" she gasped. "No way. That was mom's thing. I am not cooking anything that isn't pastry. What else?"

He shook his head. "That's it."

She hated that he appeared bored. "Well, I'm telling you that's a crock."

He tilted his head. "You don't think helping people is a good thing to do with your time?"

"I have a job."

"Which you hate."

"I don't..." she began but couldn't continue. Maestro had been her sounding board for five years. He'd been privy to her every whine and complaint about her job as a pastry chef for a large bakery that cared little for their employees. "Okay, I hate it, but it pays the bills."

"So would your mother's shop. Plus, you'd have a place to live."

"I own an apartment."

"Which has a mortgage you're struggling with." He waved a paw at the room. "This place is mortgage free."

"I don't want to live in a small town where everybody knows my business."

"No, you'd rather live in a big city where you are ignored and treated like an old lady."

Jess gasped again. Her cat had clearly recalled her sharing that little gem as well. "I don't want to talk about it."

"Fine. Would you mind opening the door? I have some business to attend to."

She wrinkled her nose and hurried to do as he asked. To be fair, he had never made a mess inside.

"I am glad you can recall that fact." He sniffed and sauntered down the steps and out to the yard.

CHAPTER

THREE

Her appetite gone, Jess forced the pie and milk back in the fridge. She had plenty to do, but the urge to go outside was too strong to ignore. Fresh air would be nice after being cooped up in the house yesterday and the car the day before that, she reasoned. The truth was she had always loved the yard best.

Down the back stairs and then exactly ten steps forward, the yard opened up before her. The flat part, where she had played on a swing and done a bazillion cartwheels, was bare except for the long grass. Maestro wasn't visible amongst the weeds, so she continued down to the garden on the next tier. Here there were mostly raised beds filled with familiar things as well as other plants she couldn't identify.

Plucking a handful of rosemary, she sniffed at her hands. It smelled better than she remembered, and a bolt of nostalgia hit her hard. How many hours had she spent planting and weeding? Not nearly as many as her mother.

She walked along the line and came back the other way then moved down to the last tier.

"You may want to take a look nearer the fence." Maestro's black ear tips peeked out between the sweet pea leaves.

"Why?"

He didn't answer, and the ears moved away. She shrugged and followed across the grass. The weeds were even longer and denser at this end, and paspalum stuck to her legs. This section wasn't a garden as such, more of a walkway. Edged by fruit trees, it ended at a gate leading into the field beyond.

"Notice anything?"

Maestro's persistence was frankly annoying, but she bit her tongue. Imagine if the neighbors saw or heard her arguing with a cat. She looked around her, but the lay of the land and all the trees and shrubs meant she was hidden from the view of any houses. The field was thankfully empty. Still, it wouldn't pay to go yelling like a crazy woman. Next thing she knew she'd be carted off by men in white coats.

"Ahem! Kindly focus, if you wouldn't mind."

Was he tapping his foot at her? She shook her head at the very idea. He was a cat and clearly did not have feet. The irony of her thoughts made her snort. "Do I notice anything? How about the weeds?"

"Anything else?"

His disparaging tone made her sigh, but she made her way to where he sat on what looked like freshly tilled earth topped with a layer of cut grass. "Do you mean this mound you're perched on?"

"Well spotted. Don't you think it looks out of place?"

Jess sniffed at his sarcasm. "I guess it does, since the

rest of the place isn't mown. Where did the grass come from?"

He nodded regally. "Very good. Now you're thinking."

Childishly, she did warm a little at his praise. "I wonder why mom dug it up only to replace it and then add grass. Usually you'd only do that to till the soil ready for planting, and from what I can see Mom didn't plant down here. Maybe she intended to, then changed her mind about it."

"You mother didn't do it?"

"How do you know?"

He actually rolled his eyes.

"She was too sick to dig?"

"Bingo!"

A prickle of discomfort ran down her back. The first she'd heard of her mother's illness was two weeks ago. Mom phoned to ask Jess to visit and had slipped it in at the end of the conversation that she was feeling poorly. Afterward, Jess told her she couldn't manage the trip because she was too busy at work. It wasn't a total fabrication.

Naturally, given their history, Jess assumed it was a way for her mother to get what she wanted. She regretted her decision as soon as she got the call from Amy Crandle that her mother had died suddenly.

The cat watched her as she worked her way through the conversation.

"Did she want to say goodbye?" The last word had a hitch in it, and Jess looked away.

"Probably that and to explain things. The urge to see you was very strong, and witches follow their urges and instincts—most of the time."

"Do you know how weird that sounds to me—how everything sounds right now?"

"I do, but we don't have time to pander to your sensitivities. With your mother gone, your powers will increase exponentially, and you need to know how to harness them before that happens."

She could hear him talking but was still thinking about her mother needing her and her refusal to come home. "You're wrong. I would have come if I'd known it was serious. Did she really understand how sick she was?"

He nodded. "Unlike you, she was a positive person. She had no intention of forcing you to come and hoped she would get better."

That smarted. Jess was known for being a glass half-empty person, but surely that was due to her circumstances.

"No, you've always been like that," he said matter-of-factly.

"Would you stop doing that!"

"I will be happy to once you get your mind on what is important."

"Which is?"

"Finding out who killed your mother."

Jess thought her eyes would pop out of her head, and her jaw fell open so far it clicked painfully. "Killed her? No one said anything about murder."

"That's because the authorities don't know."

"How is that possible if she's already been seen by the coroner?"

"The man is inept."

"And how would you know that?"

"He's old and lives on the next street over. I've bumped into him many times over my lives, and he's always struck me as a blundering oaf."

Jess closed her eyes and rubbed her temples. "My head hurts really badly."

"Mmm. That can happen in the beginning. Synapses overload and all that."

"You're not helping."

"I will help you a great deal once you've mastered some of your powers and looked at this mound."

He sounded sincere, which was different from the snarky tone he'd adopted since last night, and she felt compelled to go closer. "I guess you wandered around out here yesterday or last night and found this, but why is it so important when it's just dirt and grass?"

"Is that all it is?"

She rolled her eyes at his mysterious tone. "Just tell me what you want me to do."

His eyes narrowed. "If I did that every time there's a situation, you'd never learn a thing."

"I don't intend for there to be any more situations. Once I sort out everything here, I'll be off home."

"We don't have time for this." Maestro hissed and pawed at the earth. "Just take a look at what's in here, will you?"

Irked at his contrariness, she crossed her arms. "I'm not digging around in the garden when I've just had a shower."

"For pity's sake. I will bite you if you don't."

The coldness in his tone was marginally worse than the steely gaze, but neither matched the look of those gritted, sharp teeth.

CHAPTER

FOUR

Jess took a step back. "You're a gentle cat. You've never so much as scratched me."

"I used to be." He flexed every claw. "You are making me incredibly angry, and I promise you won't like it if I lose my temper. Your mother has a spade in the shed, so there's no need to sully your hands."

Jess turned toward the shed before she could stop herself. "Fine!" She stomped up the path to the shed and rattled the door, which was locked.

"The key should be under that ceramic rain boot by the door."

She jumped. "Do you have to sneak up on me like that?"

"It's not done deliberately. Cats are notoriously light on their feet."

Decidedly out of sorts, she glared. "It's a shame you talk so much instead. You haven't let up all morning, and I'm beginning to hate the sound of your voice and your judgmental attitude."

"You're breaking my heart," he said with no hint of remorse. "Get the key."

"A 'please' now and again wouldn't kill you," she grumbled. The rain boot wasn't too heavy, and underneath sat a large brass key. Jess pushed it into the shiny lock and turned it.

Sheds were notoriously dark and cluttered. At least that was how Jess pictured it would be. She should have recalled her mother's wasn't anything like that. Sunlight shone in from one multi-paned window and lit up one half of the room, which seemed bigger on the inside. Not Tardis like in Dr. Who, but something similar.

The other half was darker and had wall-to-wall shelves filled with old bottles. In the middle was a long thin table that held gloves, small digging tools, a tray of seedlings, and a large pot. On the left-hand side just inside the door was a rack of digging tools including a shiny spade. She plucked it from the peg and waved it at Maestro. "Happy now?"

"Desperately."

Jess fumed at the sarcasm he had down to a fine art and followed him back to the dirt pile. While Maestro sat to one side, she scraped off the grass then put the edge of the spade to the dirt and dug out a little.

"We'll be here all day at that rate. Put your back into it."

She shot him a glare. "I'm not built for this kind of work."

"Trust me, you can handle a little digging, and you'll handle a whole lot more than this by the end of your training."

As much as she was annoyed with the bossy beast, she couldn't deny that statement was intriguing. Coincidently, she did have more stamina lately when you considered her lack of sleep, which hadn't affected her at all. Good grief, was she actually buying into all this witch malarky?

Maestro smiled serenely.

Wait. Cats can smile?

He winked.

With a rude word, she put the spade into the soft earth and pushed down with one foot. It slid in easily, and she grunted as she scooped out half a spade full and deposited it near the fence.

"Again."

"Why are you ordering me around this way?"

"Because it's the only way to motivate you to get this done."

"Get what done?"

"Dig!"

She put the spade into the earth with as much strength as she could muster, and it went all the way in up to the handle. Bracing herself for the weight of the earth, she leaned in and heaved. Spade, dirt, and Jess lifted. She fell sideways and landed on her butt. The airborne dirt and spade flew downward. The blade hit the earth, narrowly missing her. She coughed and spat. Dirt covered her face and head.

To add insult to injury, Maestro was rolling in the grass and making a weird yowling sound. Weirder than him talking.

"Are you laughing?" she spluttered.

He gulped for air. "Me? Ah...no."

"You are!"

"It's just—you should see yourself. Guess you don't know your own strength." He yowled some more.

"I am stronger," she mused. "Much stronger than I used to be."

"No need to sound so shocked. I did warn you."

"Warn me?" She spluttered again and wiped her face on

the back of her hands before she stood. "You could have been more specific."

"Coulda, shoulda, woulda," he snorted.

"Is this payback for something I did to you?"

The grin slid from his face. "Possibly. More likely how mean you were to your mother."

Jess gulped and looked away, ashamed by her negligence. The truth was she had wanted to mend their broken fences a long time ago, and there had been opportunities. She simply hadn't known how to let go of her hurt and humiliation.

"Self-pity won't get this dirt dug."

His tone was gentler this time, and Jess tried again with the spade. It was better than seeing the accusation in his eyes. This time it went better, and she got into the swing of it without even a hint of breathlessness. Considering she was a couch potato when she wasn't slaving over making pies, Jess was impressed. Being a witch might have some cool advantages after all.

"Keep going."

She couldn't seem to help herself and dug out a bigger scoop and deposited this on top of the last one. After a few more, she dropped the spade. "Enough, I need a drink." A lump of dirt rolled down the mound, and something protruded from the hole it left.

"I believe you're right." Maestro padded over to inspect it. "Good job."

"What did I uncover?" Jess leaned forward to stare, wiped her eyes, and stared some more. "Is that what I think it is—a hand?"

"To be precise, it's a finger," Maestro said dryly.

She blanched. "Do you think there's a whole body in there?"

"Let's assume so, shall we? The alternative would be decidedly more gross."

Jess dropped to her knees then scampered back on her butt away from the claw-like finger poking out of the earth, which was still sliding gently away around the finger to first reveal a hand then a wrist.

Maestro was suddenly by her side. "I should have said this earlier, but keep calm."

"Keep calm? There's a body buried in mom's garden."

He nodded. "Clearly."

"But how did you know it was here?"

He sniffed disdainfully. "I could smell it, and I'm surprised you couldn't."

She gasped at a sickening thought. "It's not Mom, is it?"

He sighed. "Think about it for a moment."

"No." Jess shook her head at her stupidity while she kept an eye on the finger, which had dirty nails that looked like the owner chewed on them regularly. While the dirt could be explained, Lissa Lavender's nails were always immaculate. "It couldn't be Mom. If everyone knows she died, someone had to have seen a body. She rounded on him. "If you knew it was here, why didn't you tell someone?"

"I'm telling you."

"I meant before now." She blinked. "Oh. No one else can hear you, can they?"

"Not even another witch, unless I choose it."

"I should call the police."

"That's a very good idea."

Her head was so muddled that Jess hadn't considered the police before that moment. She felt in her pocket for her phone while her brain scrambled to think of a way to explain how she'd made this discovery. Something that wouldn't land her in jail or more likely a place for the unhinged.

CHAPTER
FIVE

Wiping her fingers on what had been clean clothes, Jess keyed in 911.

"What is your emergency please?"

"Hello. Ah, police, I guess. I found a body."

There was a slight hesitation. "Is the person alive? Do you need an ambulance?"

"Well, they're buried, so probably not."

There was a longer silence, which seemed completely understandable, and this was followed by a couple of clicks.

"Please confirm your name and address and where you found the body."

Jess did as she asked and waited some more. Maybe she really was still dreaming, and when she woke up she'd be back at her tiny apartment, and all would be right with the world once more.

"Ms. Lavender, do you know the identity of this body?"

"No."

"You don't recognize the person?"

"I only uncovered fingers—sorry, a hand is visible now.

To be honest, that's enough exposure for me. Can I go back into my house? I desperately need a drink."

Silence followed, and behind her Maestro was making something that could be a smirking sound.

"You may leave the scene, but stay available. The police will be there shortly. Please do not touch the body or anything around it. You may hang up now."

Unsteadily, she got to her feet and managed to get back to the house without vomiting. Maestro came too, watching her intently.

"You won't faint, will you?"

"Scared I'll fall on you?"

He snorted. "It did cross my mind."

"I'm okay for now."

Soon they were back in the kitchen. She gulped down a glass of water and was wondering how the body got there when a knock on the door made Jess lose her grip. The glass shattered at her feet.

"Pick it up later. The police are here."

She didn't ask how he knew. Hurrying to the door, she yanked it open and came face to chest with a police uniform and had to lean back to see the officer's face. He stared impassively down at her then flipped out a notepad. "Ms. Lavender?"

"That's me." She smiled at all that alpha male in a uniform, loving the cliche and her sudden change in fortune.

He did not smile back. "I'm Officer Fine. You reported a body on the premises."

Jess thought he was indeed fine but kept that to herself. "That's right. In the garden."

"May Officer Purdon and I take a look?"

That's when she saw another officer behind him. Much

younger, he was not as tall or quite as handsome, but still impressive in his uniform. "Sure. Follow me."

Why do I sound so bubbly? She shook her head and led the way down the hall, through the kitchen, and out the back door. "You probably know it's in the garden and that I have no clue who it is. To be honest, I didn't want to look harder than I did. He can't have been there too long, you know, with the lack of decomposition and everything." Jess was aware of, and apparently unable to stop, the chattering.

"It's a man?"

She turned around and found herself eye level with his belt, as he was on a higher step.

"Oh, I'm not really sure, but he does have big hands. I guess that's a rookie mistake—assuming things."

He stared at her as if she wasn't quite right in the head, and to be fair he wasn't wrong.

By this time, they had reached the fence, and she pointed to the mound of dirt. "There you go. As promised." She flinched. The lack of male interaction that wasn't a boss or a colleague was showing in all its glory. A dose of Officer Fine in name and looks made her positively giddy. Maybe the shock of a dead body and Maestro's mention of her mom being murdered were contributing to her losing her mind.

He knelt by the hand and using his pen lifted the closest dirty finger. "It does indeed look like a male, but we'll need to excavate for a better look and to see if he has any identification on him."

"Here you go." She handed him the spade noticing the other officer was rather pale.

Officer Fine gave the other man a side-eye before thrusting it into the dirt. "Call the station for assistance," he ordered. Then he rolled up his sleeves to reveal tanned, muscular arms. Concentrating, he carefully scraped soil from the sides like an archeologist on TV. It didn't take much effort, as once he released key areas the earth fell away to reveal a smartly dressed, if dirty, man.

If it wasn't for his paleness and the fact that he was as stiff as—a dead person—Jess could almost imagine him sleeping. "He's not very tall, is he?"

"No. Maybe 5'6". You still don't recognize him?"

"Sorry. I haven't lived here for years. I barely remember anyone, and certainly didn't recognize most of the people who came by yesterday to give their condolences."

"Condolences?" He quickly looked away, obviously embarrassed that he had forgotten. "Of course, your mother passed away a few days ago."

She heard Maestro sigh.

"Sorry for your loss," the officer muttered. "This is an odd coincidence." His eyes widened as if he was surprised that he'd said the words aloud.

Is the cat messing with the officer's mind?

"You're telling me," she said instead of mentioning what she was thinking. "I didn't know my mother was that sick, and I wasn't expecting visitors yesterday, so a body in the garden is quite frankly the last straw."

Don't get hysterical.

"I'm fine."

Now the officer looked really worried. "I recognize him. He's your neighbor. Or was your mother's neighbor."

Jess peered around him to see the face again. "What's his name?"

"Gerald Urwin."

"Doesn't ring any bells. I wonder who hated him enough to kill him."

The officer didn't argue the point about it being murder. "A few people might say he wasn't on their best friend's list. Including your mother."

She gasped. "You're not suggesting that my mother killed Mr. Urwin, are you?"

"I didn't know your mother that well, but I can't imagine it. I'm just mentioning the fact since he is buried on her land."

"Well, yes, but that doesn't mean much. If she was sick, anyone could have come on her property and buried him."

He leaned in. "If she was sick? Is there some doubt?"

"Of course not. Do you think someone killed her too?"

"Not according to the coroner."

"Then I don't understand what you're implying. Did Mr. Urwin and my mother have a fight?"

He looked a little sheepish. "Something like that. According to the files my partner sent to my phone on the way over, among other things, he didn't like the smells from her baking."

Jess couldn't help a wry smile. "Well, I can't argue with that. She did make some disgusting concoctions."

Company is coming, Maestro announced in her head.

They all faced back up the path as a car door slammed, then they heard voices. A minute later several people came down the pathway. Two men wheeled a gurney, and she was suddenly anxious about seeing the body dragged from the earth. "I'd appreciate you letting me know when you have more information."

"I can't make any promises," he said as he pulled out a camera and began taking photos.

CHAPTER SIX

A few minutes later she was being herded out of the way of the ambulance officers.

"Oh, you poor dear. Come inside and I'll make you a nice cup of tea." Amy Crandle appeared out of the blue and took Jess's arm to gently pull her away.

Since she didn't know what else to do, Jess went with her.

You better pull yourself together. That was a warning if ever I saw one.

She looked down at the cat. "A warning?"

Amy stopped in front of them. "Whatever do you mean, dear?"

"Oh, I was saying that I really need to pull myself together."

Maestro nodded several times.

"Now don't be so hard on yourself. Come and sit down." Amy tutted and continued into the house. "This is a massive shock on top of your mom passing away, and I don't usually speak ill of the dead but Gerald Urwin wasn't a nice man."

Jess glanced up to see if she was being serious. It looked that way. "Being killed for being unpleasant seems a little over the top."

"Killed?" Amy nodded slowly. "Why, I suppose he must have been. One generally doesn't dig themselves into a pile of dirt before they drop dead. Poor Gerald. If only he hadn't lost his manners."

Jess sat down at the table, staring at the woman bustling about the kitchen as if it were her own. It was more than a little odd that Amy was so accepting of Gerald being found in the garden. She gulped. Amy clearly didn't like Gerald. That was a motive if ever she heard one.

Sometime later, she was still nursing the cup of strong tea that had grown cold when Officer Fine arrived at the door.

"I thought you'd like to know that Mr. Urwin has been taken away."

"What did the coroner say?"

"Even if I knew for certain, that's not something I could share just yet."

"Cup of tea, Officer?"

"Thank you, Mrs. Crandle, but if you wouldn't mind I need a word with Ms. Lavender."

"Of course." Amy nodded and stayed right where she was. "Although, there's no reason to miss out on a cup."

He raised an eyebrow. "That's very kind of you, but I should have clarified. I need a private word. I will stop by to see you later, Mrs. Crandle. I believe you live next door."

Amy looked put out for a moment, and then an excited gleam hit her eyes. "Yes, that's right. I look forward to a chat."

He saw Amy to the door then came back to the dining

room. "I'm sure this has all been a shock, but would you clear up a few things for me?"

"If I can, but I don't know what else I can tell you. I haven't been home to Good Fortune in years, so I don't know who had a problem with my mother or with Mr. Urwin."

His eyes widened. "Why do you think the two deaths are connected?"

She bit her cheek, wishing she didn't blurb out every thought. "I'm not saying they are, but it is pretty strange that my mother is dead and now a man who didn't like my mother, according to Amy Crandle, is also dead and buried in Mom's back garden."

"I believe your mother died of natural causes."

Jess lowered her voice. "Do you think so?"

"I don't give my personal opinions, but that is what is written on her death certificate, so it will be legitimate."

"I guess."

He gave her a side-eye. "Why did you dig up the body?"

She grimaced. "I guess that might seem odd, and it wasn't my intention. I honestly had no idea there was a body there until I uncovered a finger."

"Why dig in the garden at all when you have a funeral to organize?"

Jess was stunned. She looked for Maestro, who was patting the tassels on a coffee table runner. It was hardly great timing for the cat to ignore her. "That is true. I guess I got overwhelmed and needed time out after yesterday, with all those visitors I didn't know bombarding me with questions. I saw the state of Mom's garden and thought a bit of weeding would be good therapy." She glared at the cat. "I really wish I hadn't bothered."

Officer Fine gave her a penetrating look. "Then Mr.

Urwin might never have been found."

"Um, I guess that wouldn't be good. Has no one asked about where he's been—for however long he's been buried?"

"He lived alone."

"That is sad," she said, meaning it.

"Indeed. I need your home address."

"Why?"

"It's just protocol."

A shiver of fear trailed up her back. "That seems an odd request. Unless Mr. Urwin was killed in the last forty-eight hours, I couldn't possibly be a suspect."

"That's not the purpose of my question. If you leave and we need to ask you more questions, we'll need to know how to contact you."

"You have my phone number."

"Is there a reason you don't want to give your address?"

Jess shrugged. "I'm just a private person."

He tapped his pen on his pad. "You do know I can find out quite easily."

What was it about him that made her want to keep her life a secret?

You're ashamed of it. You know you could have done more, but you were lazy and wanted to do the opposite of anything your mother suggested.

"Fine!"

He raised an eyebrow.

"Oops. No pun intended." Jess rattled off her address, glaring at the smirking cat. He knew exactly what he was doing, and she wasn't impressed.

Officer Fine caught her eye. "Is everything okay?"

"Do you mean apart from my mom dying and finding a body in the garden?"

He winced. "Fair enough. It's not easy to deal with one thing let alone two of that magnitude. I also want to let you know there are people who can help with trauma if you need it."

She smiled tightly. "I think I just need some time to get my head around everything and to get into sorting out my mother's things. Keeping busy always helps to keep the demons away."

Maestro coughed and looked away.

Officer Fine gave her a final searching look and stood. "If you change your mind about needing help, here's my card. And please stay out of the garden until we finish our investigation."

"I will, and thank you for being so kind." She ushered him to the front door, shut it hastily behind him, and threw herself on the couch face down.

"There's no time for a nervous breakdown. People need you."

"Go away. I don't need you, and I don't need people."

"Sure. And while you're at it, let's pretend you aren't a witch and I'm not a familiar."

She blew a lump of hair out of her eyes. "Is that possible long term?"

He smirked. "Not even short term. Now, stop wallowing and get down to the shop so you can check on things."

She groaned. "What kind of things?"

He avoided her eyes. "Things that are growing, steeping, and need adjusting."

"I'll be useless because I know nothing about Mom's potions."

He tapped one paw on the wooden floor, his nails clicking. "We both know that's not true. You studied with your mother since you were little more than a toddler. By the time you left you had all the rudimentary concepts of potion making instilled in you."

"Then I left town and promptly forgot everything," she told him mutinously. "Plus, there's certainly no hurry for me to go there when I'm just going to chuck it all down the sink."

He stiffened. "No, you won't. People need those potions."

"I don't care. I'm selling everything and going back to Portland."

Maestro yawned. "We'll see. In the meantime, how about we go to the shop?"

Jess rolled onto her back. The ceiling needed a paint. "Will you stop harassing me if I do?"

"For a while."

She sighed and ran upstairs to pull a light cardigan on over her dark-blue dress and picked up her keys from a bowl on the small hall table.

"Grab that brass keyring. It will be useful. You don't need car keys. It's not far."

Jess dropped her keys back into the bowl with a clatter and picked up the brass keyring, which had three keys on it. "I know where the shop is." She'd been bossed around most of her life, but having a cat do it was intolerable.

He sashayed past her. "Oh, it's not so bad. I'm a pussycat once you get to know me as only the real you can."

"Funny guy," she muttered.

"Just one of my many talents." He sat eyeing the door.

"Shame you can't open doors by yourself," she said snippily.

They headed down the path to town with a chilly atmosphere around them. Hoping it was only the weather, Jess pulled her cardigan tighter.

CHAPTER
SEVEN

Yellow tape adorned the gate and front door of the house on her left. It had to be Mr. Urwin's place. Jess shivered when she saw another policeman tying more tape to the gate at the side of her house. She hurried along when she saw the curtain twitch at the house on her right. The last thing she wanted was to get waylaid by Amy.

Maestro was right that the shop was too close to drive to, plus parking on Main Street was at a premium. Lavender's Lotions and Potions was wedged between two stores. The windows sparkled as if they had just been cleaned.

It looks like Jenny Winter is in.

"Who the heck is Jenny Winter?"

Your mother's assistant.

"Since when did she need an assistant?"

He hissed.

"Since she became ill," she answered her own shameful question.

Shall we go in before people see us chatting?

Jess glanced around, but of the few people she could see no one appeared to be looking her way. She opened the door, and a large brass bell jangled noisily, startling her. "Darn it, I forgot about that," she muttered as a young woman came out from the back.

"Sorry, we're not open today."

"The door is unlocked." Jess pointed out unnecessarily.

The woman frowned but spoke pleasantly enough. "That was my mistake. Sorry to inconvenience you."

"Is your name Jenny Winter?"

"That's right. Have we met?"

"Not that I'm aware of. I'm Jess Lavender."

Jenny's eyes widened. "Oh my! I can't believe I didn't recognize you when you look so much like Lissa. I intended to stop by to meet you last night, but there was an emergency, and I couldn't get away. I've closed the shop for a few days out of respect, and most of the town knows. I hope that was okay."

She was a little bit too bubbly, and Jess took a step back. "It's fine with me."

"Oh, that is a relief. It seemed a lot to assume, but I'm sure you have plenty to do before you're ready to come in to work. I'm so sorry for your loss, Jess." Jenny's eyes misted. "Your mother was the most wonderful person."

"Uh-huh. To be honest, I won't be working here. Actually, I'm selling the business." She ignored the death glare from Maestro. "Say, you wouldn't be interested in buying it, would you?"

Jenny paled and clutched her chest as if she'd been knifed in the heart. "Oh no, that is such bad news. I love working here, and as much as I would love to, I can't afford to buy Lavender's Lotions and Potions." Her chin wobbled, and a tear tracked down her rosy cheek. "Excuse me. I have some medicine to decant for a customer."

Disappointed in what she'd hoped would be a quick fix,

and a little unnerved by Jenny's distress, Jess frowned. "I thought the shop was closed."

"Yes, it is, but Daphne Dennison has an upset tummy and needs the potion urgently. I said I would drop some off after I checked everything." She tipped her head. "It's okay. You don't have to pay me for the time."

Awkwardly, Jess had been thinking that very thing, and she would bet their pink cheeks were a perfect match. "Does she really eat roadkill?" she blurted.

Jenny's eyes brightened and she snorted. "Who told you that? Wait, let me guess—Amy Crandle?"

"Bingo."

"I knew it! It's not true at all. Daphne is an animal lover and hates to see dead animals, so yes she does collect them from the road. She takes them back to her place and gives them a burial down the back of the plot of land she owns. It's quite sweet really."

"And people call me odd." Jess said while it occurred to her that Daphne was clearly a woman not afraid of dead things and digging.

"Do they?" Jenny asked.

"Not to my face, so don't get any ideas." Jess winked at her.

"Oh, you are funny. Your mother said you were a hoot. You're so lucky to have had her for a mom." Jenny wiped the corners of her eyes. "Some of us weren't fortunate enough to know ours."

"I'm sure it could feel like that."

"There you go again with your joking." Jenny gave a small grin before entering the back room. "It will be sad to have to find somewhere else to work." She glanced over her shoulder with a puppy-dog look. "And live."

Jess frowned. When she was a child, she had made the

upstairs her sanctuary. Surrounded by bottles and supplies, it became a place to read and do her homework as well as a place to hide away from the world—including her mother. "You live here?"

Jenny nodded. "I guess Lissa didn't tell you I was staying upstairs. It was only supposed to be for a short while until I got back on my feet, but you know how it is. I got comfortable with it being so handy to work, and it meant your mother didn't have to come in to work every day. Will you be in a hurry for me to move out?"

Jess was slightly amused by Jenny's forthright manner and annoyed in equal measure that she knew nothing about the assistant or the accommodation. It was a big thing to keep from her daughter, but then her mom hadn't mentioned dying either. "I won't be throwing you out on the streets, if that's what you're asking. I have no idea how long it will take to sell, so let's not get ahead of ourselves or plan for a long future."

Jenny came back over and hugged her. "Yay! This way I can stay and keep the place looking good for any potential buyer, and you don't have to think about that side of it. Plus, I'm always here to show people around."

"It does sound ideal." Jess just managed to avoid another hug by stepping into the kitchen area where the potions were brewed. That was a lightbulb moment. *Brewing went with witches, right?*

There you go. Maestro sat beside her feet, smiling.

"Oh my goodness! Is this your cat? Isn't he gorgeous?" Jenny swooped on him like a vulture and clasped him to her chest.

Jess laughed at the look of disgust on his face. "He obviously loves you and your snuggles. Don't you, Maestro?"

He glared, but his claws didn't protrude even slightly. Maybe he protested too much about being cuddled.

Maybe you stop being an ass and save me from this torture.

She ignored his plea. "Everything looks in order, Jenny. You clearly know what you're doing, and I certainly don't."

"That is very kind of you to say so. Ah, I don't mean to be pushy, but are you sure we couldn't keep the shop open? Just for a little longer? Obviously, with my limited knowledge I can't make up all the potions we sell, but I'm adept with the basics, and it would be revenue you'd miss out on while you wait for the business to sell." Jenny's eyes got all puppy-dog wide again. "And maybe I could have a small wage if sales warranted it."

"What do you think, Maestro? Should we let Jenny carry on with the business while we wait?"

"Oh, listen, he's purring, bless him," Jenny gushed and snuggled him tighter.

Jess did listen, and the noise he was making didn't quite sound like purring. She decided it would be churlish to refuse this when the idea of it made Jenny so happy and might get rid of some stock, thereby saving her the bother. "Then I guess that's what we'll do."

Jenny could hardly hug her with her arms full, but she beamed, and her eyes grew a little misty once more. "You're the best. Just like your mother. I won't let you down. The shop is making a healthy profit, and I will do my best to ensure it stays that way. Is there anything else I can help you with. Like the funeral?"

Jess grimaced. "With all the drama today, I haven't done a darn thing about it."

"You had some drama?" Jenny winced. "Was it Rebecca's stew? You could take some of this potion too."

"What? No. I haven't touched much of the food at all. It

was finding the body and then having to come here to check on things. The day has completely gotten away from me. In fact, I haven't even had lunch."

Jenny turned pale. "Did you say you found a body?"

With Jenny in shock, her arms loosened. Maestro managed to time a wiggle to perfection and jumped to the floor. He moved out of the kitchen, which was probably best in all respects.

CHAPTER

EIGHT

Having repeated the sorry tale of Mr. Urwin, Jess was officially exhausted, and Jenny descended into a flood of tears. She also looked angry.

"Dying is one thing, but being buried in Lissa's garden shows no respect for either of them."

Jess agreed, yet it sounded as though if it had been another garden it might have been okay. "I hear that no one liked him."

"I'm sure that's not entirely true." Jenny shrugged. "Maybe it is. He was so grumpy all the time. And he hated this shop and anything associated with Lissa."

"Really? Why do you think that was?"

Jenny leaned closer to whisper. "He said she was possessed."

"Why would he say such a thing?"

Jenny grabbed a cloth and proceeded to wipe the clean counter. "I'm sure I don't know."

She knows all right.

Jess put a hand on Jenny's. "I think you do know something, and I'd appreciate your honesty if we're going to work through this together."

Jenny chewed her lip for a few seconds then nodded. "Your mother liked to joke around the way you do, and sometimes she would put something out there that made people like Mr. Urwin feel as if she were casting a spell. It's silly, I know, but she was very good at it. So good that they —he—believed her. He even got the police involved."

Continually hearing that she was like her mother gave her an odd feeling that she couldn't discern. Was she pleased or annoyed? Maestro rolled his eyes, and she got back to the conversation. "I see. And here I was thinking Officer Fine didn't know much about my mother."

"Isn't he divine?" Jenny sighed. "Being the professional that he is, he didn't pay it much mind, but he did keep an eye on things when the tension bubbled up."

"That sounds interesting. I know he lived next door to my mother, but how else did Mr. Urwin come into contact with her?"

"Didn't you know? He was the local doctor for a few years. He moved here to work until he retired."

"How old was he?"

"Same age as your mother. Early sixties."

"No way!"

Jenny giggled. "I know what you mean. He didn't look a day under eighty. To be fair, your mom was young looking for her age. You two could have been sisters."

"I don't know about that," Jess scoffed.

"That's only because of..." Jenny waved a hand up and down the front of Jess then slapped a hand across her mouth. "I'm sorry."

Jess narrowed her eyes. "No, please go on. I'd love to hear about our differences."

Jenny backed away. "No, I couldn't possibly."

She means you dress like an old lady. You know it's true.

"I do not dress like an old lady." Jess glared at the cat.

"I'm so sorry." Jenny promptly burst into tears.

"Yes, you said that," Jess said pointedly, then the anger slipped away. Jenny seemed like a nice lady, and Jess was being unnecessarily mean. "Look, you aren't the first person to comment on my wardrobe selection. I happen to believe in being comfortable. You know what, let's forget about it."

"Yes, please," Jenny sniffed. "Your mom was always telling me to be careful with the truth in case it hurt people. I should get this lotion to Daphne. It's a bit of a walk."

Ouch.

The cat was getting on her last nerves with his snide attitude. "You don't have a car?" she asked.

"I usually use your mother's, but I didn't like to without asking."

It occurred to Jess that Jenny was the passive-aggressive type who often got what she wanted.

She is rather good at it.

Too good

Don't be so harsh. She's been very good to your mother.

Jess sighed. It wasn't like she had anywhere to go, and she had her own car doing nothing back at the house. "You can use the car for now."

"Thank you." Jenny gushed. "I'm truly a careful driver."

"I have no doubt. Well, I'll leave you to it. See you soon."

"I won't be late."

"What for?"

"We're meeting later to organize the funeral," Jenny said as though it was already a done deal. "Unless you don't want to."

Jess cringed inwardly. How had she forgotten about having to do that again? Still, maybe the assistant had more of a clue about these things. "Do you know what to do?"

"I googled it. Plus, everyone's been telling me how it should go."

Jess smirked. "That sounds familiar. This place hasn't changed one bit."

"Mostly that's a good thing, right?"

"Sure." Jess left quickly in case Jenny wanted to extoll over the virtues of this wonderful town—the place that broke her heart. "I have no idea what I'm doing."

"Most people don't. All you need to do is be open to what's coming next."

That made her take notice. "I don't like the sound of that."

"What's that, dear? The car backfiring or my creaky knees?"

Jess swung around to find Amy Crandle behind them, chuckling at her joke.

"Don't mind me, Jessica. I find that I joke more when under stress. I see you've visited the store. Isn't Jenny delightful?"

"She seems to be."

"You know, if it hadn't been for her, I don't know what your mother might have done these last few weeks."

Jess's cheeks tightened when she forced a smile. "Close the store, I guess."

Amy gasped. "We can't have that! People rely on her remedies to keep them going. Why, the rub she gives me for my knees gets me moving every morning."

"I'm sure there are lots of drugstore creams that would do the same."

"I tried them all, and nothing worked like Lissa's

lotion," Amy contradicted fiercely. "And I'm not the only one who thinks so."

"OK."

"Don't you remember when you used to work at the store how many repeat and loyal customers your mother had?"

"I mostly did deliveries after school on my bike."

"There you go. I bet that kept you out of trouble."

Jess stiffened. As a child, she'd been studious, well-behaved, and never in trouble. Was Amy alluding to the fractious teenage years, when she realized that her mother was only interested in the shop and its customers, and that trying to please her was a waste of time.

"Sorry to listen in." A deep voice came from behind them. "Is somebody in trouble?"

He looked so handsome and concerned that all her annoyance melted away and she smiled stupidly, glad that Amy had no such issue when confronted by a good-looking man.

"Officer Fine, how lovely to see you so soon. Everything okay? Did you find the murderer yet?"

"Good afternoon, Mrs. Crandle. You'll be the first to know."

Jess hid a smirk at the twinkle in his eye. "No trouble here," she said, answering his question. "I was explaining to Mrs. Crandle how I used to do deliveries for my mother on my bike and didn't work in the store, which is why I'm selling it."

"I see. Could we have a chat, Ms. Lavender?"

"You run along, dear." Amy pushed her gently in the back. "Jenny has the meeting set for 4pm, and you won't want to be late."

Jess gaped. "Where is this meeting that I know nothing about?"

"At Lissa's place. I mean, your place. I thought Jenny would have mentioned it. Anyway, when she heard from the funeral director that you hadn't been in yet, she thought we could take care of most of the details quicker if we all got together."

A delegation was all Jess needed, but Officer Fine was nodding along with Amy as if it made perfect sense. "And who else is coming to help me?"

"Just Jenny, me, Rebecca North, and Daphne Dennison."

"I see. I guess everything is decided then, and I have plenty of time to help you solve the case, Officer Fine." She stomped off down the street and didn't slow down until he touched her arm.

"I'm not sure where you had in mind, but the station is back the other way." He pointed over his shoulder.

Jess was growing tired of being ordered around. "I need coffee."

He studied her for a moment. "Sounds good to me. This place makes the best in town."

She read the sign. "Good Fortune Diner. Really?"

"It's kinda quaint," he said ruefully.

"Is it though?"

Officer Fine let loose with an attractive grin. "Let's get you that coffee ASAP."

CHAPTER NINE

He opened the door and led her to a corner table. "Will your cat be all right outside?"

"No need to worry about him. He's more switched on than most people I know, and if he gets bored he knows where home is."

"Fair enough. I'll get the coffees. What would you like?"

"A cappuccino please. Large. In a takeout cup."

He didn't comment, and she watched him make his way to the counter. Everyone greeted him. No one seemed wary, but they all cast looks of interest her way. Dear old Good Fortune. Home of gossip dripping with well-meaning. Or so they pretended.

She turned away to the window and studied Main street. It was the same yet different, and she'd just figured out why. When she was growing up, this was a drab place. Some of the shops closed and others struggled through her childhood. It began to change before she left—now every storefront sparkled and looked interesting.

Why do you think that was?

"I have no idea, but can you leave me alone for five minutes."

A large takeout cup appeared in front of her. "Sorry, this may take longer than five minutes."

Her cheeks warmed. "What is it you want to discuss?"

"Mr. Urwin had something odd in his system, and I wonder if you can tell me how that might have happened."

She almost spat her delicious coffee. "You're kidding. I'm not a doctor or a coroner, and I wasn't around when he was murdered."

A few gasps nearby told Jess that her voice had risen. She took the napkins he offered and dabbed her mouth. "You seem like an intelligent guy, so I'm guessing there is actually a sound reason for asking me, right?"

The corners of his mouth twitched. "Thanks for the vote of confidence. I heard that you worked in your mother's store before you left town." He put a hand up to thwart her intended interruption. "Now, hear me out. Even if you were simply the delivery person, I imagine being around your mother every day for even a short amount of time you might glean a certain amount of knowledge about her work. Am I wrong?"

She shifted uncomfortably. "Not entirely."

"Thanks for your honesty. I'm going to tell you what it was we found, and if you want to help take the focus off your mother being involved in his death, I think this is your best shot."

"No pressure," she muttered. "How come you aren't looking at my mother's shop if you think something in it was used to kill Mr. Urwin?"

He gave her a measured look. "Without a science degree, I have no idea what to look for, but had I known you were going there after I left you I might have."

"Having no idea that Jenny Winter was employed, I thought I should check on things, but I can't imagine I'd be any help."

"Let's test that." He pulled out his notebook and flicked a couple of pages. "Here we go. Guarana, what do you know about it?"

Jess closed her eyes and pictured the definition she'd read up on before she stopped caring. "Guarana has many potential health properties such as helping with focus and memory. High in antioxidants, it fights fatigue, soothes digestion, helps prevent blood clots, is good for your skin, may help reduce cancer, and could increase weight loss." She opened her eyes to find him looking impressed.

"And are there any downsides to taking it?"

"Plenty. It can cause insomnia, anxiety, digestive issues, irregular heartbeat, headaches, restlessness, and shakiness."

"Maybe I'm wrong, but didn't you just say some of those things were on the good list?"

She sighed. "Herbs do work, but how much you take and how you take them as well as how your body reacts to them can make them more or less effective."

"Or harmful?"

"Sure. Now tell me how he took the stuff could prove my mother's innocence?"

He grimaced. "I wish I knew."

He sounded so sincere, and she wondered if there had been anything between the two of them. That made her stomach twist a little. "You liked my mother?"

"Although I didn't know her as much as I would have liked because she was always so busy." He smiled sadly. "It seemed she was easy going, loved a laugh, and cared about people."

"Unlike me."

"Hey, I never said that."

"You didn't have to. Even though they are trying to hide it, the whole town thinks I treated Mom badly." Jess took a swig of her coffee. "Maybe I did."

He tilted his head. "Speaking for the whole town is an exaggeration. I'm sure you had your reasons for leaving."

She snorted. "A whole bunch of them," she said to his raised eyebrow. "Oh no, I am not pouring out my troubles to you."

"It might help me understand the case better."

"That's a bunch of BS if I ever heard it."

"You don't know that. If I know why you are so hard on yourself, it could give me an insight into your mother."

"Stop right now with the psychoanalysis," she begged. "You're supposed to be looking into what and who killed Mr. Urwin. Mom wasn't into retribution, and it seems to me that if all accounts are true and he really couldn't stand her, then he wouldn't have gotten the guarana from her. Would he?"

He pursed his lips. "You make a very good point."

"So glad I could help." She stood. "Are we done here?"

"You can't run away every time you don't like the direction of a conversation."

"Oh, I'm very good at running away." With that she marched out the door.

Get a dose of deja vu?

"Shut up!" Jess didn't care about the people nearby. She was mighty fed up with this whole business. And she was hungry. The thought of shopping or going back into the cafe made her itch.

Don't get angry, but I happen to know where there is plenty of food.

A vision of the full fridge and freezer wasn't appealing. She wished she'd thought to bring the rest of her coffee with her before she stormed out. She'd need a heavy dose of caffeine to cope with her afternoon visitors.

I'd be surprised if your mother doesn't have an amazing coffee machine still.

That's right. She did love coffee, and I bet there is a container of her favorite cookies in the cupboard.

She would be delighted that you ate them.

For some reason, his sincerity made her eyes water. Jess all but ran home.

CHAPTER

TEN

Just as Maestro predicted, the coffee machine was still there. It was hidden on the counter by a stack of mail—no wonder she hadn't noticed the lifesaving appliance yesterday or this morning. Her heart sank as it occurred to her that opening and sorting that mail was now her responsibility.

First things first, Jess put the coffee on and then opened the fridge. Her appetite had returned, and her stomach didn't recoil at the sight of so much food. She would eat what she liked and toss the rest, starting with Daphne's dish.

Maestro sniffed at his empty bowls. "Better leave throwing anything out until your visitors leave."

"I guess it would be more prudent in case one of them checks the trash." She glanced at the brass clock on the dining room wall. 2 pm. "Apparently time flies even when you aren't having fun."

"Suck it up, buttercup. Eat your food as fast as you can."

"What do you mean? I've got two hours."

"That will hardly be long enough to check on the dead guy's place next door and get back here."

She grimaced. "Why would I want to go in there?"

"Can you think of another way to find out how he died."

"We already know he was poisoned."

"By guarana?" He scoffed.

"Sure, if that's what the police think. Why do you care?"

"Why don't you? You heard what Fine said. It could help prove your mother's innocence. And better yet, we might find out who killed her and why."

Her appetite dwindled as she ran through a few scenarios. "Mr. Urwin was already dead and probably buried before Mom died. Because him being buried on her property points the finger at her involvement, it means someone wanted to discredit her as much as he did. We should look for proof that he had an accomplice."

"Now you're thinking."

"Jealousy is a good motive," she suggested.

"Lissa was loved by many," he said huskily.

Jess studied him for a moment. "You loved her too."

"I was fond of her, as I am of all my witches." He sniffed. "Unless they prove impossible."

"Okay." She found the container of cookies her mother loved and put her coffee in a to-go cup. "Let's do it now before I lose my nerve."

"Good girl."

"Girl?"

"Compared to me, you're not even a toddler."

"We have a lot to talk about."

He nodded warily. "When we've solved the crimes."

"One moment while I get changed."

"Whatever for?"

"So I blend in with the surroundings."

"Good grief, this isn't a movie. There is a low part of the fence down the garden that you can climb over. No one will see you going in or out."

"You do know that I'm too old for climbing," she protested.

He smirked. "You are stronger and more agile than you were two days ago. Trust me on this and at least give it a try."

She wanted to argue, but in truth she did feel—something. A lightening. Less puffed when she walked. She rolled her shoulders. No aches nor pains.

Maestro simply gave her a knowing glance and strutted to the back door. She let him out and followed him to the area of fence he'd mentioned. It had a bow in the wires, and she straddled it, hopping until she could bring the other leg over. It was actually pretty easy, even in a dress.

"Told you so."

She bent down. "Who's a clever pussycat?"

"If you rub me between the ears, I will not be held responsible for the consequences."

Her hand dropped an inch from his head. "You let Jenny do it."

"That's because she thinks I'm merely a cat."

"So you're not a cat?"

He swished his tail "I'm so much more. Now stop stalling and get inside."

Jess glanced around the yard. "Ahh, what about the police?"

"They left."

"So no one is watching the place at all?"

"Just Mrs. Crandle, and she can't see past his shed."

Jess couldn't think of any more excuses, so she followed him to the back door.

"There's a key under the mat."

"What about fingerprints?" she asked through a mouthful of biscuit.

"They've already done all that stuff."

"I don't know…"

"Look, there's a cloth over there. Use that."

"Eww! I don't know what it's been used for."

"I swear you are getting on my last nerve."

"Ditto!" Jess took a swig of coffee and placed the cup on the step before wiping her face with the back of her hand. She kicked up the mat with the toe of her shoe and picked up the key with one of the tissues stashed in her pocket—just in case she got emotional. It was tricky to turn the metal and not rip the paper, but after a few tries it clicked satisfyingly.

Opening the door, she poked her head inside. "Hello?"

"I told you there's no one here."

"It doesn't hurt to check." She crept into the kitchen. "It's very tidy apart from all these plant books everywhere."

"Not all men are slobs."

"Stop reading my mind."

"Stop generalizing."

"What I meant was," she huffed, "considering the police are looking for clues, I thought they'd turn the place upside down."

"Sure, you did. Let's check the bathroom cabinet."

"I want to check his pills over there first." She pointed to the corner of the kitchen counter where a box sat.

He smiled. "Well, well, maybe you do have some talents I hadn't counted on."

She poked out her tongue, oddly pleased that she'd impressed him. "Look at this lot. He must have every medicine on a hypochondriac's wish list."

Maestro jumped up on the counter. "Why do you say that?"

"He's got nose sprays, ear drops, eye drops, all kinds of headache pills and ten creams for aches and pains. Hmm. None of these are prescriptions, and lots of them are herbal remedies. Don't you find that odd when he abhorred mom's homeopathic way of doing things?"

"Very odd, considering he was a doctor."

"It implies that it wasn't what she sold he didn't like. It was her!"

He padded from one end of the counter to the other. "Yes, that would make sense."

Jess hurried through to the bedrooms. Two were bare and dusty. Since it had furniture, the third one must be his. It was the closest to her mother's house and looked down slightly over her mother's bedroom. A telescope stood beside the bedside cabinet by the window and pointed directly at her bedroom window.

"Eww! He was spying on her."

"It would seem so. But to what purpose?"

She shot him a disbelieving glance. "He was in love with her."

"What is your obsession with love? If that were even remotely true, the man had an odd way of showing it."

Maestro was right about Mr. Urwin in some respects, but there was something so wrong about all of this. "I don't have an obsession with love, but this," she said, tapping the telescope, "fits in with my jealousy theory."

Jess grabbed the telescope and pressed her eye to it, forgetting all about the tissues, and peered through the lens. She could see her mother's dressing table where she used to sit and brush her long hair. Even from here she could pick out a group of photos. She knew most of them were of Jess through the years. Except, right at the back there seemed to be one of a man.

"Did Mom have a boyfriend?"

"Not that I am aware of. As my connection to you grows, the one between your mother and I diminishes."

His voice was sad, and Jess felt something emanating from him—like pain.

"Let's go home." Head down, Maestro led the way.

CHAPTER

ELEVEN

Jess went straight to her mother's bedroom to check on the picture. The man was very handsome and had thick, jet-black hair. She didn't recognize him. What she hadn't seen from Gerald's bedroom was that her mother sat beside him, and he looked at her rather possessively.

"Do you know this man?" She pointed at the picture.

Maestro hissed. His hair stood on end.

"What's the matter?"

"This man has a dark heart."

"How do you know?"

"I sense it."

"Do you think he might have harmed Mom?"

"Possibly" he said in an anguished way.

"It's not your fault if he did."

Maestro didn't answer.

"Do you know where I can find him?"

"You are not to go anywhere near him."

"Look, I understand you are upset, but I have gone along with everything you've asked me to do, and you don't get to order me around without a good explanation. Even then I reserve the right to say no."

"We'll see."

"Yes, we will. I happen to know there is an animal rescue center just outside of town."

"That is in very poor taste, even for you."

"Maybe, but do you get the message or not?"

"I do." He growled. "Please do not go anywhere near this man. I sense he is dangerous, and you don't have near enough power to protect yourself yet."

She blinked. This caring side to the bossy cat was new, and it confused her. "I promise to give everything considerable thought before I do anything that might be rash."

"I guess that's the best I can hope for, but I'll leave you with one last thought. If you don't care enough about your life, just remember—if you die, I die."

"Hang on a cotton-picking minute. My mother is dead and yet here you are."

"Fortunately for me, she had already granted me to you. You have no children, so there is no natural granting available after your death. We are bound together for life and death."

A shiver ran down Jess's back. "That's a lot of pressure."

"I just hope it is enough to keep us safe." With that, he left the room.

Jess sat down on the soft bed, and the smell of her mother wafted up stronger than ever. "I hope you didn't die painfully, and I'm sorry I wasn't here." Tears spilled down her cheeks, and she blew into one of the tissues. These were the first real tears since she heard the news, and it seemed that they weren't stopping any time soon, so she lay back on the bed and let them have their way.

If only they had seen eye to eye on half the stuff they

argued about, things may have been different. If her mother had thought to mention that they were witches, at least she would have known they had some common ground. Instead, they had rubbed each other the wrong way with so much unsaid.

I thought I was keeping you safe.

Jess sat up and looked around the room. "Maestro! Was that you? It's not funny!"

He came back into the room, eyeing her suspiciously. "What are you talking about?"

"Didn't you just talk to me in my mother's voice?"

"I would never be so cruel." He huffed, then his hair stuck up. "Wait, did you hear Lissa?"

Jess glanced around the room and nodded. If he hadn't spoken—who had?

The cat gave an odd little shimmy. "Lissa's not gone."

Her stomach twisted. "Don't be silly. There's a body."

"That's not the same thing at all."

Jess put her hands over her face and rocked. "This is too much."

"It is also good news."

She sighed, more confused than ever. "How can it be good news?"

"She's left some of her presence behind to guide you to bring her back."

Her mind spun with the idea, but was it such a leap when here she was talking to a cat about being a witch? "Then why the heck isn't she here right now explaining this stuff?"

"The in-between world doesn't work that way."

She rocked some more.

Voices coming up the path made them pause the argument and heralded a knock on the door.

"Yoo-hoo!"

"Is it 4 already?" she gasped. "I can't do this."

"You must. These women may have more clues. Plus, there still needs to be a funeral. Make it for later in the week to give us all time." He looked away. "You should probably clean yourself up a little."

Not aware of getting up, Jess made her way across the landing to the bathroom. In the mirror, her face was swollen and blotchy. Wetting a cloth, she washed her face, brushed her hair, then reluctantly walked down the stairs to open the door.

CHAPTER

TWELVE

"Oh, you poor thing." Amy swooped in and pulled her to an ample bosom. "It's a good thing to let it all out. You've had a terrible couple of days, so you go ahead and cry, dear."

"Let the poor girl breathe. I'm Daphne Dennison, in case you don't remember from last night. You do look like your mother."

Released from the clench, Jess opened the door wider and nodded at Daphne, who had the huskiest voice she'd ever heard from a woman. "Please come in."

Behind the others, Jenny breezed inside with a plastic container, a clipboard, and a pencil case. "Let's use the kitchen table. I made cookies. Shall I put the kettle on?"

If Jess was a cat, her hackles would be rising at the bulldozer approach. "I'll do it. Everyone, please sit down and make yourselves comfortable."

"How are you doing with the food? Any empty containers need returning?" Daphne asked pointedly.

Amy tutted. "Give the girl a chance. It's only been twenty-four hours."

"Not yet," Jess said. "I'll return them when they are empty and clean. I promise."

"Very well."

Daphne's implied "be sure you do" was abundantly clear.

"Where to start?" Jenny leaned forward eagerly. "Lissa loved her lilac suit best. Could she wear that?"

Jess swallowed hard. "If I can find it."

"As luck would have it, it's in my car. I picked up the dry cleaning after I saw Daphne, and there it was."

Amy sighed. "How lovely. It was meant to be."

"Pure luck if you ask me."

"No one did, Daphne." Amy pointed out.

"Hmmpf! Have you been to see her yet?" asked the roadkill scraper who was clearly feeling better after her medicine.

"My mother? No, I couldn't manage it today. I'll go first thing tomorrow." Jess didn't like explaining herself. Although, it seemed like the easiest approach right now, and she was grateful to have something to do with her hands to stop them from going around Daphne's judgmental throat.

She's okay. She loved your mother.

Give me a break. I get it already—everyone loved her. They still don't get to take her death out on me.

No, you'll do that quite well yourself. Stop being so paranoid.

Jess wanted desperately to argue with him, but she didn't imagine that would go down well with her visitors, especially if she got all hand-wavy, which she was inclined to do. Their eyes were on her as they waited expectantly for the promised tea she had yet to put in the pot. She did so and brought them cups and saucers. Next she brought the teapot, complete with its handmade knitted cozy, to the table. She turned it twice to the left and then three times to the right before collecting milk in a jug.

"Sorry, there's no lemon."

"Don't worry, dear," Amy said over-sweetly.

Spare her from passive-aggressive townsfolk. Jess wondered idly if there was a plural for a group of them. Sweetly sour seniors? Except for Jenny. She bit back a chuckle as all four women sat back and waited. After precisely three minutes, she poured and was rewarded with satisfied nods. Had she just passed a test?

Maybe the biggest one yet, Maestro snickered.

"You won't want to leave the funeral date for too much longer," Amy asserted. "Your mother deserves to be put to rest."

"I've decided Friday at 11 a.m. will be best." Jess told a white lie, but it gave her a few days to get things sorted and sounded as though she had given it a great deal of thought.

I believe that I suggested later in the week.

"You'll have to check with the funeral director that they have room that day." Daphne sipped her tea noisily.

"Oh, do you think Mr. Urwin's family will be looking at that date?" Jess managed innocently.

Daphne shrugged. "There is him to consider, but there could be other deaths. You never know in a town with an aging population."

"In that case, I'll get right to it after I see Mom." The words made her shudder. No matter her cavalier approach to the funeral, or the terse words they had last shared between them, the fact remained that her mother was dead, and Jess must see her that way. Was anyone ever prepared to lose a parent?

"That sounds perfect." Wearing a satisfied smile, Jenny

wrote on her clipboard. "Now, we have the music and food to sort out."

Amy settled her cup on its saucer and looked around the room. "And the venue. Will we have the wake here, Jess?"

"No!"

The others gasped as one, and Jess licked her lips. She hadn't meant to sound so horrified.

"I only meant that I think a lot of the town will want to say their goodbyes, and the house is far too small to have everyone here."

"That is true." Amy nodded. "Everyone loved Lissa, so there will be a good turnout."

Dodging that bullet successfully, Jess was inclined to go with the flow. "I'd be grateful for any recommendations?"

Jenny tapped her notepad. "What about the community hall? Or the funeral parlor has a room they hire out."

"I haven't been in either, so whichever you ladies think will be suitable is fine with me."

"Let's keep it all at the funeral parlor and let them cater," Jenny suggested.

"I don't mind bringing something," Daphne protested.

"I'd rather you didn't," Jess said firmly. "You are all such good friends of Mom's, and I think you shouldn't have to do more than helping me organize the funeral. You need the time to grieve as well."

Maestro chuckled from under the table.

"That is so kind of you, dear." Amy sniffed into a tissue. "Jenny, I'll give you the list of appropriate food, if you could contact them and arrange everything."

"I'd be happy to. Now we just need the list of songs, which you can take your time with. And when you go see your mother, you could speak to them about music while you finalize the pamphlet. At least you know you'll be happy with that side of things."

Just as Jess's mind was about to explode, Maestro drew their attention by scratching at the back door. She jumped up to let him out, and oddly the group stood too.

"Thank you ladies so much for coming and for your help."

"You are so welcome." Jenny smiled sweetly. "I'll let you know as soon as possible whether the funeral parlor is free for Friday."

"Thanks." Jess shut the door and leaned against it.

Maestro slipped back in and sat beside her feet with his ears pricked up.

"Please don't let them come back," Jess whimpered, completely worn out.

"Not tonight," he asserted casually.

Was she completely bonkers or did this cat have the power to persuade people to his way of thinking?

CHAPTER
THIRTEEN

Peering around the side of the lounge curtain, she made sure that they really had gone, then ran upstairs. "Mom, are you there?" She called out in each room.

Maestro sat at on the top stair and watched. "I told you that it doesn't work like that."

"So how does it work, smarty pants?"

"All I can tell you is that she'll come when she can."

Jess marched into her mother's bedroom and dropped face-down on the bed. "Why does this all have to be so darn hard?" she mumbled into the coverlet.

The bed moved slightly, and his voice came from beside her. "I wish I had all the answers, but I don't. A presence stays with us for a specific reason, and I believe your mother has left instructions on how to bring her back."

The idea was both scary and enticing. "Can I really do that?"

"You're doing exceptionally well so far," he said encouragingly.

She turned her head sideways to glare at him. "Please don't with the sarcasm."

"What? You can't handle a little praise?"

She grimaced. "If I'm honest, it's not something I'm used to."

"Goodness. We're most definitely not descending into a pity party on my watch."

"I was merely explaining."

"That's all right then. You may have noticed that while I take my job seriously, there is a limit to the level of commitment I have on a personal level."

"Does all that mean you don't like hugs or any affection?"

He shuddered. "Not particularly. Humans can be rather rough or persistent. Either way it makes me want to bite them."

"I'll be sure to remember that should I ever feel the urge to hug you again."

"Now we're getting somewhere."

"Hah! To me it feels like we aren't moving an inch. I have no idea what I'm supposed to do—about everything. I know the bossy brigade has a plan, but I won't know if it's going to be okay until the day."

"A funeral is much like anything else. There is a beginning, a middle, and an end. I assume you know where to start by saying something nice. The middle usually takes care of itself and then we are left with the end. Ashes or buried?"

"Good grief! I don't know."

"Didn't you and your mother talk about anything of significance when you were together?"

"That would be a firm no." She gave him a side-eye,

which was easy from this position. "And if you are who you say, and you've supposedly spent years with both of us, then surely you would know that."

"I don't spend every moment hanging on witches' words." He huffed. "I do have my own lives to lead."

"Lives?"

Maestro rolled his eyes. "Oh please, everyone knows a human's cat has nine lives, and it stands to reason that a familiar would have a good deal more."

Jess blinked. "How many more?"

He pursed his lips, which was kind of cute. "Can we get back to the matter at hand? You'll either have to ask her friends or make a decision based on your knowledge of your mother."

"I don't want to discuss anything with anyone in Good Fortune, and I just told you that Mom and I didn't discuss anything of significance. Maybe it's written in her will."

He stood. "Now that is a very good point. Get your body off that bed and down to the lawyer's."

"Right now? I don't even know who that is?"

"It's a small town. How hard could it be to track down a lawyer?"

"True. Are you coming?"

"You find the address, and I'll meet you there."

She stretched and smoothed her dress. "When do I get my magic?"

"What did you want it for?" he asked suspiciously.

"Well, if I could fly, I wouldn't have to hunt the lawyer down. I could zip across town to every lawyer." She snapped her fingers. "Just like that."

"And that demonstrates perfectly why you ease into it and don't get all your powers right away."

"I'd use them wisely."

"How is it wise to drop in on the people of this town who don't believe in things that go bump in the night and scare the daylights out of them?"

"I'm not exactly a scary witch."

"Just the word witch will drive the people of Good Fortune into a frenzy."

Jess was mid-sigh when she remembered she already had the lawyer's details. Where was her brain? She ran upstairs and picked up the pile of mail she'd dumped on her Mom's dresser. Sure enough the top one was from Maddren Law. Mr. Theo Maddren sent his condolences and invited her to the will reading on Thursday.

Maestro peered over her shoulder. "We should get down to his office now."

"But it's late. Surely they'll be closed."

Maestro touched the paper. "I believe he has some business to take care of, so he's working late."

"How did you check when you've been right here all afternoon and you didn't know where his office was?" She snapped her fingers. "I was right...you do have powers."

"They are limited to gentle acts of persuasion." He bowed. "Well done for figuring it out."

This time, his praise was somehow incredibly uplifting, and tired as she was, she slipped on her shoes and followed him back to town.

It was a warmer evening tonight, and several neighbors waved from their front steps. Yesterday she would have ignored them. Today she waved and smiled. Her step faltered. That was odd. Nothing had changed. Her mother was still dead. Her cat was still a familiar, and she was apparently a witch.

"Don't think about it right now," Maestro said.

"Think about what?"

"Why you feel so calm."

Which only served to make her think of exactly that.

CHAPTER
FOURTEEN

The young receptionist sniffed and dabbed her eyes with a handkerchief when Jess explained who she was.

"I'm Holly Jones. It's lovely to meet you, and I'm so sorry about your mother. Let me check if Theo is free."

She knocked on a wooden door and slipped into the room without closing it. Maestro followed her.

"Sorry to bother you, Theo. Lissa's daughter is here to see you."

There was a slight pause before a pleasant voice answered. "Excellent. Please send her in."

"Right away. Oh! Hello, kitty, aren't you a cutie?" Holly reappeared holding Maestro to her face and nuzzling him between the ears. "This little boy must be yours?"

He looked so wretched that Jess wanted to laugh. "He certainly is. The big baby doesn't like to be left at home by himself."

Molly dropped him into Jess's arms and then held the door wider. "Aww. How sweet. Go right in, Jess."

"Thank you."

The lawyer rose from a sturdy oak desk and held out his hand. "I'm so sorry for your loss, Ms. Lavender."

He turned out to be a bit of a silver fox and not some stuffy suit.

"Thank you, and Jess is fine."

He smiled. "The official reading of the will is tomorrow morning. I was about to call to make sure you knew that since I wasn't sure my letter to your home address would have had time to reach you."

"I didn't receive it, but I found the letter you sent to mom's place today. I had a question, if you don't mind, about mom's wishes for her funeral. I have no idea if she wants to be buried or cremated. It probably could have waited, but I'm going to the funeral home tomorrow morning and thought I could organize that at the same time."

He nodded. "I understand. She would like to be buried."

"I guess you already knew that from the will."

He smiled. "And we were very good friends."

Jess squirmed. Theo seemed a little young for her mother. "I see. How long were you together?"

"Pardon?" Then his cheeks turned a fetching pink. "Oh. No, we really were just friends."

Jess laughed. "Sorry, I misunderstood."

He grinned back. "That's not a good thing for a lawyer to hear. Can I help with anything else?"

"Well, I'd like to know more about mom's last days and who she spent them with, if you know and have time."

He leaned back in his chair. "May I ask why?"

He'd said it gently, but she thought she detected a touch of censure. Despite this she was drawn to be honest. "I have a feeling that her death wasn't cut and dry. I know that sounds crazy, since she was so sick, but there is also the fact that a body was found in her garden."

"Ah, yes. Mr. Urwin. Very tragic. Although, I don't follow how the two things are connected."

"The police are concerned that my mother killed him."

He laughed. "Sorry, that wasn't professional, and I know it's not a joking matter, but your mother wouldn't hurt a fly. I've known her for a long time, and she made it her life's mission to make the people around her feel well and happy."

"Was there no one who wanted to hurt her?"

"Not that I know of. I daresay she had people like Mr. Urwin who didn't approve of her potions, but as a person she was adored by most."

"Unlike Mr. Urwin."

Theo shifted in his chair. "He moved to Good Fortune from a large city for a quieter life and to retire, but he never seemed to be happy here."

"Do you think he was in love with my mother?"

His eyes widened in horror.

"Yes, I know it seems an odd question when you've said he didn't like her, but I don't think the two things are mutually exclusive," she went on.

"I sense you have a reason for asking."

"He has a telescope set up in his lounge that looks directly into Mom's bedroom."

"Ahh. I wish I hadn't heard that."

"I know...it's gross."

"Have you told the police?"

"Not yet." She grimaced. "You see, I went to the house when I shouldn't have."

"Can I assume that I am your lawyer going forward?"

Jess frowned. "I hadn't thought about it. Why?"

"If I am, then what you've just told me is covered under attorney-client privilege."

She nodded enthusiastically. "Then, yes, you are."

He steepled his fingers, and his mouth twitched. "Now, as your lawyer, I think it prudent to tell the police about it."

That was not what she'd expected. "They might put me in jail."

"That's not likely."

"Still..."

"Our department is top notch, and it wouldn't surprise me if the officers had already checked on the telescope. However, I also know that any piece of evidence is instrumental in each investigation. Do you want to find out who killed Mr. Urwin and possibly your mother as well as exonerate her?"

Jess shuddered. "I would. Something's not right here, and a murderer on the loose in Good Fortune isn't good for anyone."

"I agree. Would you like me to come with you?"

"Would you? That would be fantastic." Immediately she felt better.

"Let's head over to the diner."

She hadn't expected a dinner invitation. "Shouldn't we go to the station first?"

He laughed again, and it was a nice sound.

"Officer Fine eats at the diner most nights, and I figure he won't mind us all having a chat."

"I wouldn't like to spoil his meal," she hedged.

"Then how about we grab a bite while we wait for him to finish?"

It sounded so feasible, and yet Jess felt awkward. It was almost a date, and they'd only just met. Still, she was hungry. "Okay, but we go Dutch."

"Of course." He nodded and grabbed his jacket from a rack by the door. "After you."

CHAPTER
FIFTEEN

Officer Fine was seated by a window, a half-eaten steak on the plate in front of him as he read a book. He glanced up as soon as they entered and watched them head his way.

Theo nodded to him. "Hey, Brodie, could we disturb you after dinner?"

"Sure." Officer Fine pointed to the chairs beside him. "There's plenty of room. Take a seat now if you like."

"We were about to order," Theo explained.

"I don't mind sharing the table—unless you'd rather be alone?"

It was a question, yet underneath, Jess heard a challenge. If it wasn't a laughable idea, she could almost imagine they were fighting over her.

"We're not together," she insisted. "Well, we are, but it's not a date or anything. We only met today, so it's just business."

Both men studied her, and she looked away, deciding that they could sort out who was dining with whom between them.

"In that case, take a seat if you'd like to."

Jess deliberately took the seat opposite him, which meant that Theo had to sit beside Officer Fine no matter which chair he chose. They sat there awkwardly for a moment until the waitress dropped off a couple of menus.

She eyed the group with interest. "I'll be back in a short while to take your orders."

"Thanks, Trixie," Theo said.

"Any recommendations?" she asked the men.

"The steak is always good, and so are the lamb racks," Officer Fine suggested before forking in a mouthful of meat.

The plate, even half-eaten, looked huge, and Jess had a hankering for something fresh. When Trixie returned, Jess ordered the chicken and avocado salad while Theo chose the steak and baked potato.

By the time the food came, Officer Fine was done and they had discussed weather and her trip from Portland.

"Don't hurry with your meals," he insisted. "You two eat and I'll finish my book."

Jess was glad about that because she was starving. She'd picked at food since she arrived and hadn't eaten a decent meal for days. The salad was everything she craved, and she ate like no one was watching. Except they kinda were.

"It looks like you enjoyed that," Trixie stated when she came to clear the plates.

"That was absolutely delicious."

She winked. "I'll tell the chef—which happens to be me mostly. I guessed you are Lissa's daughter, and we took bets that you wouldn't need any food for weeks."

"That is so true, and I am thankful. In fact, I feel guilty for not eating at home."

"Don't you give it a thought. Just tell those ladies that

you enjoyed everything before you dispose of it. Trash day down your street is tomorrow." She winked again and took an armful of plates back to the kitchen.

Jess looked around to check no one had overheard, then turned back to the men. "I don't suppose either of you would like to take some of that food off my hands?"

They both laughed and shook their heads.

"The last thing you need is for that group to see you handing out their food. Better do as Trixie said and chuck it out." Theo grinned. "At night."

"It's such a waste."

"But a whole lot safer, if you get my meaning," Officer Fine said with a twinkle in his eye. "Now, what was so important that you wanted to see me tonight?"

Jess glanced at Theo, but he merely nodded. Darn it, she'd hoped he would broach the subject of her trespassing. She took hold of the closest thing, which happened to be the pepper mill and proceeded to make a mess on the gingham tablecloth.

"Surely it's not that bad," the officer said gently.

"It isn't good. I'm afraid I went into Mr. Urwin's house this afternoon."

He raised an eyebrow. "It has tape across both doors."

"I saw that."

"Yet you ignored it."

"Mmm. You see my cat..."

"Carry on," he urged when she went silent.

"He, um, thought he saw something inside," she said, completely invested in her story and with no idea where it would lead. Who said confession was good for the soul?

"And you followed him, right?" Theo prompted.

She nodded. "Just in case it turned out to be the murderer or a clue."

Officer Fine was not amused. "Unless he's grown opposable thumbs since I saw him earlier, I'd conclude that you actually opened the door."

"I did. You see he was crying and scratching to get in, so I knew it was important. He and I have a good rapport."

"He speaks to you?"

She gave a tight grin and crossed her fingers in hopes that he was an animal lover. "Don't all animals speak to their owners?"

He raised that eyebrow again. "So they say. I think it's more likely that the opposite is true."

"You may be right," she chuckled, knowing he didn't comprehend the truth of his words. "Anyway, he was through the doorway in a flash, and I followed him to a bedroom. Beside the bed was a telescope. It was pointed at my mother's bedroom. I looked through it, and it was like being in the room."

Officer Fine screwed up his nose briefly, and she was pleased to see he didn't like it any more than she did.

"I appreciate you coming to confess, and while I'm not happy about what you did, I guess you and your cat didn't do any harm. Just don't do it again." His eyes twinkled. "By the way, the coffee cup was a bit of a giveaway."

"Darn it!" How had she forgotten to pick it up on her way out. "I hoped no one had noticed, but I guess you went back to the house some time after I was there."

"We often return to the scene—that's why we put up tape to deter everyone else. By the way, my people know their jobs, Ms. Lavender. The telescope direction was noted."

She felt silly, thinking she could put anything over on him and knew he was enjoying her discomfort. "Everyone is capable of overlooking things."

"I can assure you that doesn't happen in my department. But what did you hope the news would do for Mr. Urwin's case?"

That perked her up. "I'm thinking that he had a crush on my mother and someone found out. They decided to do something about it, killed him, and disposed of the body in Mom's garden to point the finger at her."

"That is a tall leap from finding a telescope."

"Everything seems a tall leap from where I'm sitting." If only they knew about Maestro and her supposed magic! "With a killer loose in our community somewhere, I assumed any clues would be dealt with as if they were the only clues. Am I wrong?"

"In this case, not entirely," he said ruefully.

She leaned forward. "Do you have any leads?"

"It pains me to admit that, no, we don't."

Jess sat back and sipped her latte. "I guess it all comes down to who hated Mr. Urwin."

"I'm not sure anyone did."

"Come on. Someone must have noticed he was perving at Mom and potentially other women."

Officer Fine glanced at Theo. "No one has mentioned anything like that concerning him."

"Have you spoken to everyone?"

"I don't have unlimited manpower," he growled. "It's a slow process, but we have spoken to many people in the community."

"Perhaps you need to look at a specific group within it."

"A group? As in…?"

"Middle-aged women. Mom's friends? They live close by and look good for their age."

"Let me get this straight. You think a woman killed him?"

"Probably not," she admitted. "He'd be heavy to lift, plus they had to dig a hole." Jess looked out the diner window where a tractor rolled from view. "Unless they had help."

"Another killer?" he mused.

She ignored that. "Maybe an accomplice. With machinery."

The officer shot another look at Theo, who was watching her with admiration. At least she imagined he was.

"The fence wasn't broken, so machinery couldn't get in the back yard," Fine protested.

"Some could. A tractor with a digger arm could reach over the fence, dig the hole, and then fill it in a very short space of time."

"And how would you know that?"

"I was born and grew up in that house. It backs onto fields that get tilled, sown, and cultivated by machines."

Officer Fine stood, his eyes wide. "That never occurred to me. I need to speak to the owners of that land."

"And the companies who hire equipment if they don't use their own," she added perhaps a little smugly.

He nodded several times. "Thank you for coming forward."

In police mode, it was clear she was being dismissed, but she had to clarify one thing. "So I'm not in any trouble for going inside Mr. Urwin's house?"

He looked down at her. "As long as you didn't touch or remove anything, I think we can overlook it. This one time."

She didn't need a degree in tone to understand he was warning her, but it was difficult not to give herself a high-five right that minute.

Let's not get ahead of ourselves.

She glared out the window where Maestro peered through the glass. "Party pooper."

Theo's eyes widened. "Sorry?"

"Oh, not you. I'm thinking about the funeral on Friday. I hope all this business with Mr. Urwin doesn't spoil it."

Wow, she was getting to be a good liar.

CHAPTER
SIXTEEN

Theo walked out with her after they paid for their meals. "Thanks for letting me tag along," he said, amused. "It was very informative."

"Thanks for coming with me. Officer Fine can be a little intimidating."

"Brodie? He's one of the good guys, as long as you don't cross him." He laughed. "You came close."

"I did, didn't I?" she chuckled. "I don't mean to, but this tracking down clues business is a long, drawn-out thing."

"You've only been in town a couple of days. Did you really think it would all fall into place so quickly?"

"I had no idea there were any murders before then, but I just figure that a man was missing, no one knew about it, and Mom died suspiciously, so there should be more urgency what with the funeral on Friday."

"Do you want my opinion—not as a lawyer?"

"Sure."

He smiled gently. "You need to let your mother's death be what it is. Talk to the doctor if necessary, but I don't believe she was murdered. Unlike Gerald. He had a lot of people riled up with how he treated Lissa. It could have been almost anyone, but whoever did it left no evidence, and I think that means you are safe."

She chewed her lip. "Unless I do anything to annoy the murderer—and how would I know what that might be?"

"I know what I said sounds a little dismissive." He smiled gently. "But you seem nice enough, so I wouldn't worry about that too much."

She couldn't help grinning. "My cat wouldn't agree with you."

"How can you say that when he follows you everywhere?" he asked, eyebrow raised.

She looked behind her where Maestro waited in the shadow of a shop. "Hmm. Say, do you feel like a walk?" When his eyes flashed with interest, she wished she hadn't asked.

"What did you have in mind?"

"I'd like to check the field behind my house for tire tracks or any kind of disturbance."

"Ahh, I get it. This is all about your theory about the digger."

"I think it's worth a look in case Officer Fine didn't take me seriously."

"Don't you worry. He'll be looking into it."

The statement was firm, and Jess believed he meant it. "Okay, so what do I do now?"

"How about I walk you home and you try to get a decent night's rest. I'm sure you have things to do and think about before Friday. By the way, be prepared. Every man, woman, and their dog will be at that funeral, and they'll want to talk to you."

She blanched. "I am so not ready for that."

"Trust me. Nobody ever is."

She nodded, and they set off for her house. It was then that she realized she had almost accepted her fate. She was actually considering living here and didn't know how to feel about that. How could her world have turned so upside down in such a short span of time?

True to his word, Theo left her at the door. Grateful he hadn't pressed to come in, she wandered around the house touching her mother's things. Regret and guilty feelings about her inability to solve the crime made her restless, and she went outside into the back garden.

Her ambling took her back to where Gerald had met his demise.

"No, that wasn't here," Maestro informed her. He sniffed the air.

She sniffed too. There was something she could smell that wasn't usual, but she had no idea what it was.

"His death is what you can smell. It is fainter now that he isn't here, but it would smell differently if this place was where he died."

Oddly she found this interesting. Her nose twitched as if she were suddenly more aware of smells in general. She turned to face back up the path. "What's that sweet smell?"

"Someone was here."

They scampered up the path to the shed. The door was ajar. Warily, Jess poked her head inside. At first nothing seemed different. Then she saw it. "Someone's wiped down the counter."

"And the cauldron."

She looked around and then gasped. "Oh, you mean the pot! I didn't pick up on that when we came in before. Maybe whoever killed Gerald made the potion that killed him here and wanted to ensure there was no trace of evidence."

"You can't be sure."

"That's just it, Maestro. For some reason I can't explain, I am sure."

He grinned.

CHAPTER

SEVENTEEN

She had one day to do everything, and first on the list was visiting her mother. Visiting. That was an odd way to think of it, but she couldn't contemplate going to the funeral home in any other way. She had never seen a dead person. Her grandmother died young, and she knew nothing about her father.

It hadn't bothered her too much until she was a young teenager. Not having other family was hard. There were no family get togethers in the holidays. In fact, they had never been out of Good Fortune that she could remember, and that was why she had left town as soon as she could. In truth, it was only one reason.

Maestro left her alone, and she appreciated that as she got ready and made her way into town heading for the funeral home.

"Good morning, Jess. You might not recall, but we went to school together."

Jess thought she recognized the large smile of the woman at reception. "Melanie Hargreaves?"

"It's Melanie Peters now. Goodness, you haven't changed a bit."

Jess wanted to say the same, but it would be a lie. Melanie still had that super bright smile but looked every day of forty-five. The black skirt and blazer did nothing for her pale skin, the observation jolting Jess into glancing down at her own bland clothes.

Her school friend had been a sweet girl despite her parents owning the funeral home, which would have given Jess nightmares. "So you took over the family business? I recall how kind you were to everyone when we were young. I imagine people love seeing your friendly face here."

Melanie dimpled. "Aww! That is so nice of you to say. I do like to think I help the grieving the way my parents did. Are you ready to see your mother? Jenny dropped off the clothes, and Lissa looks lovely."

Since her feet didn't seem to want to move forward, Jess could only nod.

Melanie smiled knowingly. She tucked an arm through Jess's and pulled gently. "It's only natural to struggle with the viewing, but it is an important part of gaining closure, and I'll be with you every step."

They went through a door in the corner of the room and found a shiny open wooden casket on a large table no doubt designed for this purpose. One foot at a time was slow going, but eventually they reached it. Jess took a deep breath before looking down.

Her mother lay sleeping. At least that was how it looked. Jenny's choice of outfit was perfect, and Lissa looked the same as the last time they had been together—not a day older. It wasn't so weird now. Yet, something was off—a ripple in the air across her mother's body confirmed it. Startled, she glanced at Melanie who merely smiled.

"Okay?"

So she hadn't seen anything odd. "Yes, thanks."

Melanie frowned, perhaps picking up on Jess's confusion. "Jenny said she had the okay to choose this coffin, but it's not too late if you don't like it."

Jess licked her lips. "No, it's fine. Just right."

"Wonderful." Melanie beamed. "Shall I leave you for a moment?"

"No!" Jess squealed before taking a deep breath. This would be her only opportunity to try to find any clues about her mother's death that might not be visible to an undertaker. Though the idea of touching a dead person, even if it was her mother, made her squeamish. "I mean, yes, please."

Melanie patted her shoulder. "I'll just be outside that door if you need me. Take as long as you need."

Jess nodded and made sure she was gone before turning back to the coffin. The ripple was still there. She reached out a hand to warily touch it. Nothing happened, except her hand passed right through it. She couldn't feel anything. It was as though it didn't really exist.

"Maestro?" she whispered.

Just ignore it.

"But what is it?" She heard him sigh.

Nothing to concern yourself with right now.

Jess did not like this one little bit. She leaned over the coffin and studied her mother's face. "I wish I'd known about your health, Mom. And about this other stuff. I feel lost." As she said the words, a lump caught in the back of her throat. In truth, she had felt lost most of her life.

Don't trust anyone except Maestro.

Jess jumped a foot back. That was not Maestro's voice.

You need to go along with the funeral.

"Are you still alive, Mom?"

Almost. The potion was strong, but I knew I would be poisoned and took something to combat it. You need to get to the shop and follow Maestro's instructions to the letter.

"And then you'll come back from wherever you are?"

Nothing is certain, my sweet girl.

She's always called her a girl, and this was the first time it didn't irritate Jess. "What if I mess up?"

You? Never.

There was a faint laugh before the ripple disappeared.

"Don't go! I have so many questions."

"Oh dear." Melanie hurried to her side and wrapped her arms around Jess. "That is a perfectly normal reaction. We all want more time. Though it sounds trite, that is why a funeral is so important. People will tell stories, and you'll glean so much more about your mother's life and how happy she was."

Jess extricated herself as gently as she could. "I'm sure you're right. Thanks for making Mom look so nice. Here's a list of songs I know are her favorites. Jess thrust a sheet of paper at Melanie and backed away."

"It was my pleasure, and your mother needed little help from me to look this lovely. Would you like to check a mock-up of the pamphlet that Jenny suggested?"

"If Jenny chose it, I'm sure it's just fine." Just when Jess wanted to cut and run, something popped into her mind. "Do you know if Mom had a boyfriend?"

Melanie blinked. "As far as I know, she had no one serious, but most of the men in town would have liked the chance. The shop was her focus as well as helping people. I guess she didn't have much time for a relationship."

Jess felt a familiar pain as Melanie's description unintentionally matched that of Jess's childhood. She had always been well down the list of her mother's priorities.

She forced a smile. "It may seem silly, but I saw a picture of a man and wondered if he was someone special who didn't know about her passing."

"I understand. It's hard to think that someone would miss out on saying goodbye, but honestly if it was someone from around here—they'll have heard by now."

"Good to know. Thanks so much. I guess I'll see you tomorrow."

Jess left for the shop, childishly relieved her mother didn't have a boyfriend, and frustrated that she was no further along in finding out who the killer was. She'd clutched at straws hoping that an old photo might reveal all, and there were still no other clues.

CHAPTER
EIGHTEEN

Maestro was already at the door, and once inside they found Jenny stocking shelves with Soothing Soap. Yes, that really was the name of it.

"Hey, Jess. How did it go?"

"With my Mom? Great. Thanks for organizing everything. It meant I had little to do really."

Jenny waved her thanks away. "It was a team effort, and as long as you're happy that's all the thanks we need."

Jess couldn't think of anything else to say about that. "I need to use the potion room."

"You do? That's great news. What are you planning on making?"

"Oh, just a little sample I've been thinking about for—giving yourself a boost."

Jenny pointed to a stand nearby. "We do have some tonics already if you need something now."

"Actually, I feel like doing something with my hands to —you know—keep busy."

"I understand. There's plenty to do out here, so go for it.

Although, it's best if the cat doesn't go in there. He could contaminate things."

Maestro hissed.

"Good grief." Jenny gasped. "It's like he understood me."

Jess gave an awful fake laugh. "He can sense when people don't want him around."

"Really? Clever cat." She knelt. "It's not that I don't like you, sweetie. If any fluff gets into the lotions, it could make people sick if it reacts badly with the ingredients. We don't want that, do we?"

Maestro turned away and flounced to the door. *There's a window in there. Open it for me.*

"Looks like he's headed home." Jess dry laughed again. "Well, I'll be in there for a bit. If you don't mind, I don't want to be disturbed."

"Sure. Your mom was the same way when she was brewing. I'm so glad you want to get involved, Jess. Perhaps you won't sell the business after all."

"We'll see." Jess hurried inside so she wouldn't have to witness the pleading look on Jenny's face a moment longer. Hopefully, she wouldn't have to make a choice about closing the shop—if her mother helped her to brew something to stop her from being dead. Was that even a thing? She pondered the odd question as she opened the window to let one grumpy cat inside.

"Contaminate indeed!"

"She means well—isn't that what you said?" Jess smirked.

"Oh, so you can remember that but not to phone your mother."

Jess grimaced. "Hey, that's a low blow."

He ducked his head. "Yes, it was. I'm sorry."

She hadn't expected an apology and suspected by his mannerism that he didn't offer them often. It made things decidedly awkward. Jess coughed. "No problem, we're both a bit stressed. How do we start? Is there a recipe somewhere."

"You can stop looking. There isn't one written down for this. Wash your hands then grab the cauldron."

She stood up from peering in the lower cupboards and drawers and shook her head. "You are kidding me. We have a cauldron here?"

"You're a witch, aren't you?"

Clearly, he was over his embarrassment. It also sounded like this was getting serious, and her nervousness grew.

"I'm not totally convinced that I am a witch."

"Still?"

She put her hands on her hips. "Tell me what I have done so far that is any way witchy?"

"Let me see," he drawled, "you talk to a cat—and hear him talk back—sometimes in your head and sometimes not. You talk to your dead mother and see the ripples of time."

Her eyes bugged. "The ripples of time? Is that what was hovering over Mom?"

"It was, and you shouldn't dismiss that ability lightly," he scolded. "Not all witches, or familiars for that matter, can see it."

Jess let that sink in for a moment. "So I have a special talent. Nice."

"Your special talent is potions."

His hiss wasn't as daunting as it had been a day or so ago, and she had the urge to make him suffer a little more. "But the time thing sounds so much better. Cooler even."

"It is not better."

"But it is cool, right?"

His eyes narrowed menacingly. "Why are you behaving like a child?"

"Honestly?" She shrugged. "Teasing you is the most fun I've had in years."

"I'm so glad I can amuse you. Now, can we get back to the task?"

The cauldron, and it really looked like one, unlike the one in the garden shed, sat in the far corner of the counter. On Maestro's instructions, Jess pulled it out until it sat on an element. She groaned.

"What's the matter now?" he asked.

"I imagined it would be hung over a fire pit or at least in a fireplace."

"Yes, that wouldn't draw attention, would it? Now put a hand on either side of it and look inside."

Jess wanted to argue, but her curiosity proved too much. The inside wasn't even a little smoke-stained. In fact, it looked like it had never been used. "What am I looking at?"

"Be patient and keep looking."

She dutifully scanned each inch. Nothing. Wait! A blue pinprick of light came from the very center at the bottom—and it grew then thickened until it was a mist. The mist turned into a fog as it hit the rim, and Jess moved back a little.

"Put your hand into the cauldron."

"I don't think so."

"Now."

She couldn't take her eyes from the eerie mist, but his command was enough to override her fear. With a hard gulp she slipped her hand inside. Her fingers brushed against something, and she attempted to pull her hand out, but it was as if something held her there. Her fingers folded around whatever it was—hopefully something without teeth.

The mist dissipated, and in her hand was a piece of wood.

"Is this what I think it is?" Jess lifted it carefully out of the cauldron. "A wand?"

"You'd be an odd witch without one. Now, drop that bushel of Lavender into the cauldron, point your wand inside, and repeat after me."

"Lavender come soothe the souls
who lie in wait
to meet their fate
and hope to rise again."

Haltingly, Jess said each word, and a tingle rushed through her body from fingertip to fingertip, and head to toe. She felt exuberantly alive as she followed his instructions to add other ingredients. Some she knew and others she had no idea about, but each felt right.

"Let only those deserving mercy
claim the right to live.
The others must face their end
with nothing left to give."

Her voice rose of its own accord with the new words as her hand rose with the wand.

"Repeat the verses three times," Maestro ordered.

As she did, the mixture bubbled and changed color until it was a deep purple. The smell was sweet but not sickly, and in the instant she finished the last line the bubbling ceased.

"Quickly spoon as much as you can into that glass vial and stopper it immediately."

She hurried to do as he instructed and slammed in a cork with satisfaction. "We did it."

"Let's hope so."

Jess didn't like the uncertainty in his voice. The cauldron was magically clean again, so all she had to do was return it to the corner and wipe down the counter after putting away the ingredients.

She glanced at the clock and sighed. "I guess we better get to the lawyer's to hear the reading of the will."

CHAPTER NINETEEN

"Theo is expecting you." Holly smiled and led them toward the lawyer's open door.

He stood and motioned her forward. "Good to see you, Jessica. And the cat, of course."

Jess smiled, shook his hand, and sat opposite him. "Maestro's still feeling out of sorts since we came to Good Fortune, so I let him follow me around."

Theo eyed the cat. "He does look grumpy, poor thing."

The fluffy black tail swished.

"Just ignore him. That's what I do when he's being obnoxious."

Maestro glared at her.

Theo laughed then coughed and straightened a pile of papers that didn't need it. "Right. Let's get to the will."

It was hard to listen to the preamble when all Jess could think of was that she might have somehow prevented this outcome.

"To my daughter, Jessica Lavender, I leave my house and all my possessions. I also leave her my business, Lavender Lotions and Potions, and the building it operates within. There is a condition to the latter. Jessica must work in the store and keep Jenny Winter on as an employee. Also, Jenny must be allowed to live above the store for as long as she desires. Should Jessica not wish to run the business, then it and the building will resort to Jenny Winter.

He put the paper down and looked up. "That's it. Do you need me to clarify anything?"

Jess shook her head, not sure how she felt about the development. Basically, her mother was blackmailing her to stay in town. A few days ago, Jess was planning to put the house on the market and go back to Portland. Her new talents made her question that. At least here she had a ready-made cover in the business.

"As a beneficiary, you are entitled to a copy of the will."

She was about to refuse, but the whole business with Jenny irked her. That, and the fact that her mother had gotten exactly what she wanted if she stayed. "I would like a copy."

"I'll arrange it right away. Is there anything else I can help with?"

She shook her head and stood. Jess had questions all right. But only Officer Fine would have the answers.

"I'll see you tomorrow," Theo said. "Meanwhile, if you need anything at all, feel free to get in touch."

He saw her out, looking concerned, and she wondered if he also thought it odd that Jenny, who had known her mother for all of a minute, stood to not only gain a business, but a building, including an apartment.

She marched down the street to the police station. Officer Purdon manned the desk and greeted her with a smile.

"Ms. Lavender, how can I help you?"

"I need to speak to Officer Fine, please."

The young man hesitated. "Let me check if he's available."

Jess paced the waiting room while Maestro, who had been oddly silent, curled up on the long-padded seat.

"Ms. Lavender, you wanted to see me?"

"Do you have time for a private word?"

"Is it about the case?"

"Potentially.

"Come this way." He led her to a decent-sized office and pulled a chair to his desk and went to sit behind.

She knew nothing about police, but it did appear that Officer Fine had some seniority. Impressed, she perched on the edge of the seat and leaned forward. "How long has Jenny Winter been in town?"

"About a year and a half."

"That long?"

"Maybe a little less. Why?"

Jess explained the will and was rewarded by his wide-eyed surprise.

"So you think it strange too?"

"I admit it surprises me, but perhaps your mother thought you needed a little push to stay."

"I get that, but it is darn infuriating."

His mouth twitched. "I can imagine."

"So you don't think Jenny did anything underhanded to get included in the will?"

"Jenny?" he said skeptically. "I can't see her being that manipulative."

"Hmm."

That noise made his eyebrow dance a little, and she looked away. Perhaps Jenny had learned her manipulative ways from Jess's mother, but Officer Fine seemed to have bought into the innocent persona Jenny portrayed.

"Are you implying that Jenny had a hand in Mr. Urwin's death?"

"Surely she is a suspect, right? I mean, with her knowledge of plants and all, it stands to reason she would be."

"Naturally she was questioned."

"And?"

"And I have concluded that the possibility is unlikely."

"I see. Did you come to the same conclusion regarding my mother?"

Leaning back a little, he steepled his fingers. "Your mother was sick."

"What if she was given something to make her sick, just like Gerald Urwin?"

He frowned. "According to the toxicology report, there is no evidence of foul play in your mother's case, and nothing was proven with Mr. Urwin."

There was no way she could bring up what she knew. "Maybe you didn't look hard enough."

"I understand that you are upset, with good reason, but I can assure you the police have done everything possible to get to this point."

"Hmm."

"Was there anything else?" he said stiffly.

He obviously thought she was paranoid, and maybe she was. "I guess not."

"Then I'll see you tomorrow."

She sighed. It sounded as though Theo was right about the whole town turning up.

Her heart hurt and her hands ached for the familiarity of the one thing that made her truly happy.

Where are you headed? Maestro demanded.

None of your business.

Excuse me?

She groaned. *If you must know I'm going to bake tonight.*
You need a good night sleep.
I need to bake.

Something in her voice must have told him how much she really did need this as his voice disappeared, and when she got outside he was nowhere in sight.

Good. She wanted to be alone. To not think about tomorrow and to bake something that made her feel good.

"Pies. Cherry jelly pies." She nodded to a couple on the street who eyed her warily. This talking to herself was going to get her into trouble if she wasn't more careful, but right now she didn't care.

CHAPTER
TWENTY

The next morning, the sun, peeking around the edge of the curtain Jess hadn't closed properly, woke her earlier than she would have liked. She sat up, scrubbing her face with her hands when it hit her. Today she would make her mother wake up. At least that was the plan. She jumped out of bed, a hot mess of emotions.

Maestro was nowhere to be seen.

After a shower, she dressed carefully in a black skirt and shirt and slipped into low black shoes. While blow-drying her hair into some semblance of order, her hand stilled in midair. Today she looked more like her mother than she ever had. Her hazel eyes were much greener now, and the lines around them and her mouth were less defined.

With an effort, she put that to the back of her mind, applied the usual bare minimum of makeup, and went to find Maestro.

He sat by the back door and didn't meet her eyes.

"Is everything okay?"

"Please open the door."

She hurried over. "I wonder why Mom never put in a cat door?"

"Because other beings might use it."

He said this so matter-of-factly that it took a moment or two to sink in. Before she could ask him any questions—she had a ton of them—he was gone. Surely he meant other cats. Beings didn't make sense. And if they were an actual thing, she didn't really want to know about it today. Maybe not even tomorrow or the day after that.

She made a pot of tea and sat at the counter to drink it. Breakfast wasn't something she could contemplate, and a little later when Maestro returned he walked right by his bowl. He looked nervous, which made her nervous.

When a knock on the door came, they both jumped. It was Amy. Unable to think of doing anything else and biting back a sigh, Jess opened it.

"Good morning, dear. I thought I would keep you company until the funeral."

"Thank you, that's very thoughtful." Jess smiled...until she saw the group coming down the path.

"Morning," Daphne shouted.

Jenny waved. "It's a beautiful day. Your mom loved the sun."

"She did," Jess agreed, blocking the doorway. "Let me get my bag so we can go."

"It's a little early," Daphne noted.

If they thought she was entertaining them this morning, they could think again.

Rebecca nudged Daphne, who winced.

"I guess we can walk slowly."

Maestro followed Jess and watched her collect her things. She tucked the vial into a handkerchief and then into a pocket of her bag. He nodded, and she followed him back down.

They turned left out of the gate and went past Mr. Urwin's house. Jess shuddered.

"When is Mr. Urwin's funeral?"

"Later this afternoon," Amy told her. "It is unusual with the crime not solved of who disposed of his body that way."

Jess winced, and Jenny turned pale.

"It's a busy day in Good Fortune," Daphne said. "Probably won't need to cook dinner."

Rebecca nudged her again.

"What? It's the truth."

Jess shifted awkwardly. This little group was determined to enjoy their outing, but she was nervous. How surprised were they all going to be when her mom woke up? Which begged the question, how would they explain it? Or would there be some kind of brainwashing?

Maestro huffed behind her.

What was his problem? The longer his silence went on, the more her fears grew. If the arrogant and usually confident cat was troubled by the outcome, that told her a lot.

They were the first ones at the funeral home, but others began to trickle in not long afterward.

Theo Maddren arrived with Holly, and right behind them came Officer Fine. Both men wore dark suits and looked very smart.

She greeted them all, the ones she knew, and the strangers who knew her mother. Her heart raced as she willed the time to pass so she could deliver the potion.

Do it now.

"Now?

If you wait any longer, the coffin will be closed. Follow the hall. You won't be seen.

"Excuse me," she said to Amy and the other women around her. She made her way to the restrooms and glanced around her. Just as Maestro had said, the hallway leading to the side room where her mother should be waiting was empty. She ran along it and pushed the door open a little to check no one else was inside.

Jess slipped inside and made her way to the coffin. Everything looked the same. As per Maestro's instructions, she pulled out the vial and unstopped it. Holding it over her mother's face, she tipped two drops on each of her eyes. Two more on her lips and on both hands.

"There." She muttered with satisfaction.

Her mother remained still as the liquid disappeared.

According to Maestro, it was now a matter of time. She checked her watch. The funeral was due to start in twenty minutes. Not wanting to go back outside, she walked around the room to study the stained-glassed window, which let in a rainbow strip of light across everything. To her right another door was ajar. This must lead back to the other side of the funeral home, where she had entered yesterday. She peeked inside.

Another coffin sat in the middle of that room.

Curiosity made her cross to it. Sure enough, Mr. Urwin lay inside, decked out in a brown suit of dubious age. His shirt was frayed at the cuffs, and his tie was truly hideous. A sort of mustard color, it was faded in patches, and she hoped he never wore that when he was seeing patients. His hair had been pushed back but looked in need of a cut. In contrast, the coffin was quite nice.

A moth rose from the satin lining and hovered over Mr. Urwin's face. She shooed it away, the back of her hand accidentally brushing his cheek. It was cold, and she jerked back. Her hand caught his hair and flopped over his eyes.

With a shiver of revulsion, she brushed it back before racing back to her mother.

"Hurry up, Mom. I need to get out of here."

Lissa opened her eyes, making Jess squawk a little.

"You're alive," she blurted. "I'm so glad you're okay, but how do we explain this to everyone?"

Lissa Lavender's eyes shone, and her mouth quivered. "There is no need, sweetheart."

"Oh, I wondered if you have a spell that makes them forget. Or do we go back in time and stop it from happening?"

"No, my darling child." She sat up. "I'm not alive."

"What?" Jess pointed. "Look at you—you're moving."

"Touch me."

Jess frowned. "This is silly," she said and reached out to take her mother's hand. Her hand went right through. She blinked. "Oh no, you're still dead?"

"Pretty much." Maestro was suddenly at Jess's side.

"You knew it wouldn't work, didn't you?" Jess accused.

"Let's just say I had my doubts," he admitted.

Tears filled Jess's eyes. "You made me believe it would be okay."

"Trust me. I wanted it to be."

"Trust you? I've done everything you asked of me since you blindsided me with this whole witchy thing. What was it all for?"

"Shhh, dear. He did as I instructed," her mother crooned.

"But why try if you couldn't come back?"

"There truly was a slight chance. Unfortunately, you haven't reached your full powers yet, so the potion was less effective. I am in an in-between state."

Jess gasped. "Are you saying this is my fault?"

"Not at all. It was all just bad timing. I was weakened and didn't pay Gerald enough heed."

"Gerald?"

"That would be me." Mr. Urwin entered the room and strolled toward them. Only, his feet didn't quite touch the floor.

"How did this happen?" Lissa asked Maestro, all gentleness evaporating from her mother's voice, hard steel taking its place.

The cat stared at Mr. Urwin in horror. "I don't know." He turned to Jess. "Tell me you didn't touch him."

She swallowed hard. "I.."

"You did! Why would you do that?" he screeched.

"It was an accident. Anyway, how could me touching him cause him to become—whatever he is?"

"You must have spilled some of the potion onto your fingers." Lissa said sadly. "It's okay."

Maestro hissed. "No, it isn't. He cannot be here."

"Maestro," Lissa warned.

He hesitated then nodded. "Jessica, we need to get the funeral started and act as if nothing is amiss."

"How do we do that without a body?"

"I'll be in here until the grave," her mother said as if this was a normal occurrence. "Afterward I'll come home."

Jess shook all over. "I don't think I can go through with this."

"There is no alternative now," Maestro said in disgust.

"What about him?" Jess nodded at Mr. Urwin, who was smugly watching them.

"Get back in your coffin," Lissa demanded. "We'll talk later when the funerals are done, otherwise you will not get any further than you are now."

That wiped the smile off his face but not the glint from his eyes. "What if I don't want to?"

"Really? You want to find that out now?" Maestro hissed.

He backed up with a scowl then gave Lissa a nasty grin. "You can bet we'll talk later."

"I thought this was where I'd find you." Melanie stood at the door respectfully. "Can we bring your mother out now, or do you need another minute or two?"

"No, we're done here," she said tonelessly.

Melanie looked around in confusion then smiled. "Oh, how sweet. Your cat came to say goodbye."

"They were very close."

"Aww." Melanie clipped the doors back, and four burly men in suits came in to carry the coffin.

In a clearly rehearsed movement, they lifted the coffin lid, settled it on the top, then stood to one side while Melanie turned the clasps and gave the lid a tug. The men lifted the coffin onto their shoulders and lined up behind Melanie, who nodded at Jess to precede them.

CHAPTER
TWENTY-ONE

Jess had to admit that the funeral was rather nice. Several people spoke, including Amy and Daphne, about how Lissa was always there to help and had made them feel better with her clever potions. The latter being quite humorous in her droll way.

Then it was Jess's turn. She hadn't spent as long over her eulogy as she would have if she'd known that her mother wasn't coming back to life. Guilt for her inability to fix pretty much anything since she got home, on top of the normal amount of guilt she carried daily, made her voice husky.

"My mother was a good person, as you've all attested to. We had an interesting relationship because we are so different, but people are like that, no matter if you are family or not. It has no bearing on how much you are loved and how much you love a person. Mom loved Good Fortune, her friends, and me." Those words came from her heart and were new additions. The truth in them nearly made her break. She bit her lip quite hard and managed to continue.

"She wanted the best for me and always gave her best to everything she did. She wanted people to be happy, and her store is a tribute to that. I know she will be missed by us all. Thank you for coming and please enjoy the refreshments next door as we celebrate Mom's life rather than mourn her death."

Maestro sat at the door and nodded to her. *Well done. Just keep it together for a little longer.*

That was easier said than done when it felt like the whole town wanted to commiserate with her and tell stories of Lissa Lavender's life. Another time she might be able to hear them, but her mind wandered. How did everything go so wrong? She'd almost accepted her mother's death until Maestro had filled her with hope. She had ruined the one chance entrusted to her, and though she wanted to rage at both of them for not preparing her for this outcome, there was an overwhelming sense of sadness at the waste of time.

After all these years of fighting to keep her independence and even ignoring her mother's wishes, she found herself desperate to have her mother back in her life. She could have been a better daughter. She should have tried harder. Her independence wasn't worth this. An ache in her throat at unspent tears made it hard to swallow.

Jenny came across the room and took her arm. "Thanks again, everyone. I'm taking Jessica home now."

"She is very pale. Are you going to pass out?"

"Daphne!" Amy scolded.

"What? Are you going to catch her if she does?"

Amy ignored her. "Off you two go. I'll make sure everything is sorted here before I leave."

Jess could only nod and allow herself to be led away.

Back at the house, Jenny used her own key to get inside

and escorted Jess to the couch. "You sit down and rest up. I'll make us some lavender tea."

"No!"

Jenny blanched.

"Sorry, I've had enough of tea." She didn't add that Lavender tea seemed completely inappropriate.

"Of course. Shall I bring you some water instead?"

"Perfect."

Jess flopped back against the cushions. She was such a failure.

"Here you go."

With a sigh, she took the glass from Jenny and gulped it down.

"Would you like to be alone?" The concern in the woman's voice was touching.

"Do you mind?"

Jenny smiled gently. "Not at all. Give me a call later if you want company. Otherwise, I'll see you tomorrow."

Waiting until the door closed behind her, Maestro hopped up on the couch and stared across the room.

Lissa appeared in a semi-transparent form and smiled. "That was a lovely funeral—so many people saying such kind words."

"How can you be so calm? If I had known ahead of time what to do—or not do, you wouldn't be dead right now."

"Don't be angry, Jess. We can never be certain how things will turn out. Had I noticed Gerald nearby, I might have thought to mention not to go near him, but I didn't know he was there."

Her mother seemed confused by that, but Jess couldn't help commenting on what happened. "Still, it seems a pretty important thing to mention about not touching anyone."

"Not anyone. Just dead people," Maestro stated.

Jess shuddered and fumed some more, though she wasn't sure precisely what her anger was directed at. If she had known all the circumstances and come home when her mom first phoned her, there might have been something she could have done to prevent her death. And if so, she would never have been put in the situation of making a potion she didn't know how to handle.

"Stop the pouting," Maestro growled. "There were plenty of reasons not to tell you things sooner."

Jess waved a hand at her mother. "I can see one reason you should have."

"Recriminations and self-pity will have to wait," her mother interrupted. "We don't have much time."

"Time for what?" Jess asked.

Lissa grimaced. "Before Gerald arrives."

Jess turned to the door, which was silly since he wasn't likely to knock. "He's coming here?"

"Undoubtedly."

"I don't want him here."

"You don't have a choice." Maestro sneered, still clearly angry with her.

Lissa tutted. "We need to make a potion to send him back, and we better hurry."

Jess followed them to the kitchen, where Maestro pointed to a cupboard.

"We need the cauldron first."

"Are you sure I can do this right?" she asked as she placed the cauldron on the bench.

"We'll soon find out."

"Maestro, be nice," Lissa warned, pointing at the cauldron. "Inside you'll find a book that only you and I can read.

On the second to last page is the recipe we need for eternal rest."

Jess opened the book, which was written in gibberish, but as soon as she placed a hand on the page it morphed into real words, and a wand appeared beside it. She had so many questions, but clearly now was not the right time for them.

With their help she found all the ingredients in a corner cupboard, which she was pretty sure held other things when she'd looked in it before. Somehow this cupboard was much larger inside than it should be, upon inspection. Following the instructions, she managed to get the mixture boiling quickly and held her breath, willing it to work.

"Okay, it's ready," Lissa said over her shoulder.

Filling a vial that also hadn't been there a few minutes ago, Jess stoppered it and held it out to her mother. "Now what?"

"Now we prepare for Gerald."

Jess looked up at the clock. "His funeral was set for two hours after yours. By my calculations, we have about an hour left—if that's how this works."

"Well done! You're right. He can't get out of there until the coffin is delivered to its resting place."

"I didn't have that part figured out, but I realized you didn't arrive here until we got home. I kept looking for you and guessed that's how it would be for Gerald."

Lissa nodded. "Excellent deduction. Your skills are coming to you a little at a time. They'll be helpful when you're assessing people's needs at the store."

Jess blinked. "Ah, about that..."

"No time," Maestro urged. "We need to get next door and find something of his that will bring him to us."

"Like what?"

"You'll know it when you see it."

Jess was not at all certain about that since she couldn't comprehend fully what was going on now. Still, if it could fix things then she had to try.

They entered the same way as last time, and for the second time Jess noticed the library books on herbs. His garden was tidy and only full of herbs with not a vegetable in sight. She crept down the hall to Gerald's bedroom.

Lissa went to the telescope and frowned. "I knew I should have kept a closer eye on him."

"Why didn't you, Mom?"

"Because I wanted to believe he was harmless and had some good in him." She shrugged. "It's a failing of mine."

"Why does he hate you so much?"

"It all started when I refused to date him."

Jess's face screwed up. "I don't know why I'm so horrified when it was so obvious." She nodded at the telescope.

"Yes, he was obsessed, and that kind of false love leads to a troubled mind."

"He tried to discredit your store by accusing you of false advertising, but did he ever hurt you?"

Lissa looked away. "Just once."

Her mother's sadness was apparent, but there had been a look of guilt. "Mom? Did you kill Mr. Urwin?"

She shimmered. "Not intentionally. I was so shocked that Gerald would touch me that way, and then I got angry when he wouldn't stop. I sent a wave of power through his body which threw him to the floor. I could have handled it better—I should have."

Jess gasped. Figuring her mother had something to do with Gerald's death didn't make it any easier to hear that she was responsible. "The thing that troubled me was that he didn't have a mark on him."

Lissa nodded. "At the last moment I cushioned his fall. Unfortunately, the shock he took caused his heart to stop and when it started again I guess the pressure was too much for him."

Jess had a sudden mental picture of Gerald flying across the room. "You mean, because he had an aneurism and shocking him caused it to burst?"

"Exactly." Lissa wrung her hands. "I truly didn't know he had anything wrong with him."

"Except for the stalking," Maestro growled.

"Except that," Lissa agreed.

At least Jess could understand that. "Sorry, but I have to ask—why bury him in the garden?"

"It was a rash decision I immediately regretted. Whatever he slipped into my tea that day clouded my judgment. I knew a few minutes later that he'd added something that I couldn't detect, which is the first time I had experienced such a thing. Without knowing what it was, I didn't have time to make and test enough antidotes before I succumbed."

"So he did kill you!" Jess's anger grew, and she had the urge to throw something, but the police might return. "I saw all the books on herbs in his house. He must have been working on it for some time."

"Years is my guess. You know the saying, 'a little knowledge is deadly.' Well, that certainly applied to Gerald. He hated what I did, but ironically in the end he wanted the knowledge that I had."

"He wanted to be a witch?"

"At first he liked to bandy that about, but I think it was more to scare people off from buying from me than a true belief about what I was. What he wanted was power—by any means."

"I guess he knows the truth now, what with the whole not-quite-dead thing going on," Jess said dryly. "But I'm thinking that non-witches can't get powers."

"That's right. You are either born with them or not, and it is genetic. Fortunately for us he doesn't know or believe that. Now let's get the place ready for his arrival."

Jess ran around the rooms doing as her mother and Maestro ordered without so much as a pout. This was her chance to make things right, and she was determined not to slip up this time.

A pungent odor of mothballs slapped Jess in the nose.

"He's here." Maestro whispered.

CHAPTER

TWENTY-TWO

Something shimmered in the light by the kitchen window and then the killer appeared.

"Hello, Gerald. We thought we would welcome you home. What can we do to make you comfortable?" Lissa asked sweetly.

His eyes narrowed. "For a start you can tell me how to get back into my body."

"Oh, that's not possible, so it won't do you any good to try."

He grew uncertain. "And why not? You're a witch after all, so I know you have something for it."

Carelessly, she waved a hand across her body. "Don't you think I would have done it by now, if I could?"

His eyes narrowed. "I want you to find a way or I will destroy your shop and your daughter's life anyway I can."

"You really haven't learned a thing about all this business, have you?" Lissa's eyes shone in an unpleasant way. "Never mind. You'll soon be out of your misery."

"What do you mean?" he hissed.

"Your body is being cremated as we speak. If only you

hadn't put that in your will. There is no coming back for you."

He shrieked, which was an awful sound, and Jess covered her ears as he reached out for Lissa—and his whole body went straight through hers.

"Noooo! You're not saying that I am stuck like this forever?" he shrieked again.

"Forever is a long time," Lissa agreed and glided into the sitting room. "But maybe there is something that could fix that."

"Why did you kill my mother?" Jess demanded, encouraging the switch of his attention to her.

"She stole everything from me. My patients were blinded by her promises and turned against me. I would have worked with her, but she refused to share her knowledge."

"How could she when you're not a witch."

His eyes ran over her. "Since you're her daughter, you must be a witch too."

Jess shrugged. "I'm still using training wheels, so there is no point in trying to get any information out of me. In fact, I only found out right before I discovered your body that I was anything but a middle-aged baker."

"I should have left you dead and buried," Maestro muttered.

Shocked, Gerald wavered between the three of them, his body flickering red, orange, and black. And Jess saw something else. He was deeply afraid that his gamble hadn't paid off.

"Come sit beside me, Gerald, and let's talk about our future." Lissa patted the couch in what could only be termed a suggestive manner. "It might not be the one we hoped for, but we can still have some fun."

Gerald's eyes shone greedily. "We're equals now, aren't we? You can't make potions if you can't touch the ingredients."

"That is true. I am sad about that, but perhaps we could do some good in the world as ghosts."

"Or make some trouble?" He winked. "Nothing too bad, but like you said we could have some fun."

While they chatted, Jess got herself into position to his left and pulled out her wand from her sleeve, hiding it at her side.

"What are you doing there?" Gerald asked.

"I was wondering if I could have some of your herb books now that you won't be needing them?" she asked casually.

He shrugged. "If you help me make up my potions, then you can have a couple."

"What about this one?"

She dropped a heavy book onto his lap, one that had been read many times and held copious notes. It fell through to the sofa. "Oops. Let me get that." She reached across him and touched him with her wand. "Tied to death, untied to life," she commanded. A purple lasso wrapped around him and held tight.

"What are you doing!" He tugged at the lasso but couldn't grip it.

Jess took out the vial and removed the cork one-handed. She threw droplets over his face and more on his hands.

Gerald unleashed a mighty roar when the liquid hit his skin. The bottle flew across the room and smashed against the wall.

Lissa made a strangled sound and glided across the room. She shook her head sadly. "It's gone."

Meanwhile, Gerald was yelling. "Something's happening to me."

Sure enough he was losing shape and becoming more transparent.

Lissa smiled softly. "Just relax. This is how it is supposed to be. No more anxiety that you're not good enough. Close your eyes and sleep, Gerald."

He tried to yell again, but nothing came from the space where his mouth had been, and soon his face was gone along with the rest of him.

"You did it, Jess." Lissa beamed. "I am so proud of you."

"But you're still here. There was no potion left for you. I'll make some more," she said in a rush, horrified that she had let her mother down yet again.

"There's no point," Maestro growled, and turned his back on Jess.

"What does he mean?"

Lissa sighed and pointed to the clock. "The time is up to make amends. I cannot come back to life, and I cannot go to the grave this time."

"Gerald can't come back, can he?"

"Never."

Jess had a traitorous thought. "So now you can stay here with me?"

"For now." Lissa raised an eyebrow. "If you would like that?"

Would she after all they'd been through in the past? "Yes," Jess said emphatically. "I can't think of anything I want more. Unless you were alive."

"Then that's what I'll do." Her mother gave her a sly look. "There is one condition."

"You're already making conditions?" Jess groaned. "Okay, hit me with it."

"You must stay in Good Fortune and work at the store, as per the will, but I need you to find a way to be happy there. What I do is very important and there is no one I trust more than you to continue my work and being happy will make everything you make more potent."

Oddly, it did make sense, but the pressure made her skin itch just a little. "What about Jenny?"

"She's a dear, but she isn't you and she doesn't have your capabilities."

Jess's heart swelled pathetically. "Fine. If that's what it takes to have you around, I guess I can move home and work in the store, but please don't get your hopes up about my potion making."

Her mother chuckled. "The only way is up, and you've done well so far."

"Speaking of homes, we need to get out of here before we're caught trespassing." Maestro sniffed the air. "Jess, you better clean up that mess first."

She quickly did as he asked and dumped the glass and cloth in the trash bag back at their cottage. When they got inside, she put the coffee machine on. "Mom, I've been thinking."

"Uh-oh." Maestro grunted.

Jess glared at him. "As I was saying, Mom, earlier you mentioned that you had to stay here for now. Does that mean there is still a chance you can live again, or are you talking about..." She shivered. "...eternal rest?"

Her mother chewed a ghostly lip. "After all you've been through, I don't want to give you false hope, but I can promise you that I will try. Every year will present a new opportunity for a witch ghost to return or leave. It is fraught with danger, and the person wishing to change can choose to try to come back, leave for good, or stay as they are."

At that moment, she couldn't read her mother's desire. "What will you choose?"

"Lets' see how this year goes, and then we can decide together."

"That would be a first." Jess teased. "But I do like the sound of it."

EPILOGUE

Jess sat at the diner watching the Good Fortune lack of hustle and bustle outside. She chuckled to herself. The small town wasn't exactly a hive of activity even on a Saturday, but there were a steady flow of people greeting each other and chatting in the middle of the footpaths.

"How are you today, Ms. Lavender?"

She looked up to see Officer Fine beside her wearing jeans and a t-shirt. She hadn't seen him come in to the diner and smiled in delight. "I'm pretty good, but unsure if it's appropriate to say so the day after mom's funeral."

He nodded. "Your mother wouldn't want you to be miserable."

"That's what I think." She wrapped her hands around her cappuccino. "Do you want to take a seat and keep me company?"

He looked pleased. "Sure, I've got a coffee coming too."

They both stared out the window some more.

"It was a lovely funeral," he said after his coffee arrived.

"I guess with so many people it was overwhelming for you."

"I did find it a bit much, but once I got home and rested, I found that I felt so much better." She shrugged. "Maybe it did help—the closure."

"Maybe, but I'd say time would help more than well-meaning acquaintances," he mused. "Have you come to terms with how your mother died so suddenly?"

His voice was so gentle that she smiled again. "I have for the most part. I was carrying so much guilt and then I figured that mom always forgave me and I knew I forgave her. That was a very cathartic moment."

"We all wish we could make amends after the fact. Guilt makes for a rocky path that never goes anywhere." He laughed suddenly. "Sorry, that's a bit heavy."

"No, I absolutely agree. Do you think Gerald Urwin is sorry for what he did?"

His eyebrow shot up. "You mean for harassing your mother?"

She nodded.

"Let's hope so. We were all getting fed up with his treatment of her and his snide remarks about her being a witch."

Jess choked on her coffee and he patted her back. When she could manage to speak she thanked him. "Wow. I can't believe he would say that. He must have been crazy. How did he really die?"

The concern for her was replaced with a certain amount of caution. He looked around them. "It was an aneurism. He'd had it a long time. Maybe from birth."

"So, it was like a time bomb waiting to go off?"

"That's exactly how it was."

"Will you still keep looking for whoever put him in mom's garden?"

"Absolutely. That's why I'm not advertising anything to do with his death, but I thought you should know the truth. While they didn't kill him, burying someone is a crime and if they're capable of doing that for whatever bizarre reason —well, let's just say I'll be keeping an eye out for weird behavior."

"Thank you for putting that to rest." She gave an embarrassed laugh. "You know what I mean, and I promise to keep it to myself."

He grinned. "I trust you."

She was easy in his company until then. That statement made her very uncomfortable. She already knew about Gerald from her mother, but Officer Fine could never know the truth about Jess, or her Lissa. Maybe it would be better if she kept away from him.

His eyes twinkled. "I was wondering, if you managed to dispose of all the food yet?"

"Shhh!" she put a finger to her lips. "I did, but that has to be our secret."

"Of course. And if that is the case, perhaps you could have dinner with me tonight."

Jess glanced around the room and several people averted their gaze. "Won't people talk, Officer Fine?"

"There is nothing surer than that. Does that bother you?"

Did it? It had been a long time since she had let a man get close and had come to expect them to let her down. Officer Fine may well fall into that category, but if she approached one or two dinners with no expectations it could be fun. Fingers crossed everything would go smoothly for a while. At least until next year when they could try again to bring mom back.

Aware that he was waiting for her answer she smiled.

"Slightly, but I'm game if you are."

"I am—on one condition."

"Gah! You sound like my mother. What's the condition?"

"How about you call me Brodie?

"I can do that, Brodie."

"I'll pick you up at seven—Jess."

She watched him leave and imagined she wore a silly grin. So much for wanting to keep her distance. It seemed that Officer Fine had cast a spell on her.

She wondered if he liked pies.

THANK you for reading Witchy Awakening, Book 1 in the Midlife Potions Series. I hope you enjoyed it.

If you did...
1 Please help other people find this book by leaving a review.

2 Join my newsletter at https://dl.bookfunnel.com/s7ae15d3fx for new releases and great deals.

3 Come like my author Facebook page at https://www.facebook.com/authorcaphipps.

4 Visit my website caphipps.com to see all my books and pick them up a little earlier.

5 Keep reading for an excerpt from book 2, Witchy Hot Spells!

Witchy Hot Spells

Jessica Lavender is a reluctant witch!

Her ghost of a mother, and Maestro, her cat familiar, have high expectations for this unhappy ex-baker.

The potions Jess makes can heal or hurt and she still has her training wheels on when another death draws her into the mystery around it.

Can Jess solve the crime and help a friend prove her innocence without revealing her talents for sniffing out murderers?

Chapter One

The smell from the cauldron wafted over Jessica Lavender, who sniffed appreciatively. This was a good batch. Making potions couldn't compare to baking, but she was beginning to enjoy it.

Maestro curled around her ankles and jumped up on a chair, specifically set at a height so he could peer over the counter.

"Did you know that mint can ward off evil?"

The cat's fancy tone always made her smile. His superior and often bossy attitude was another matter.

"I do, but that's not why I made it today. Daphne Dennison has been complaining about her stomach again." She snuck a peek at him.

He smirked as she knew he would. "Remember when you thought she ate the roadkill she collected?"

Jess chuckled and shook a finger. "Don't pretend that you didn't think so too." After a couple of months back in her home town of Good Fortune, she was beginning to get to know the people in her mother's life. It had been reported that Daphne ate roadkill when what she really did, due to a soft heart, was take the poor dead animals home and bury them in the large plot of land she owned.

Maestro snorted. "Well, it did sound rather—eccentric."

"Name one of mom's friends who isn't just a little eccentric?"

"Jenny Winter."

"Hmm." This was her go-to answer when she couldn't think of something appropriate and didn't want to be rude.

"Surely you don't still suspect her of nefarious undertakings?" he grumbled.

Jess decanted the potion into a glass bottle and stoppered it. "Look, I like Jenny. Her sweetness sets my teeth on edge occasionally, and maybe it is all genuine, but if I hadn't stayed in Good Fortune she would have inherited Lavender Lotions and Potions, as well as this building, which includes her apartment. Doesn't that strike you as a little too coincidental?"

He tutted. "We both know that Lissa's next-door neighbor, Gerald Urwin, killed your mother with a slow-acting poison that was undetectable until it was too late. Jenny had nothing to do with that or Gerald's untimely death. Besides, your mother wouldn't have been put in that condition about you selling if she hadn't been worried you would leave town the minute she was buried. You know that would have seriously impacted your witchy abilities."

"I know that now," she huffed, "but I still don't get how Gerald could have drugged Mom. She refuses to discuss it, but Mom knows smells. So how did he manage to get her to drink a potion?"

"Why don't you ask her?"

"Hah!" Though her mother was dead, Lissa Lavender was not exactly gone. Due to a mix-up with a life-restoring potion, her ghostly presence stayed at the family home and couldn't leave. It was a sad situation, and Jess was mainly responsible, thanks to a lack of knowledge and power. This was an ongoing battle. "You and Mom are still keeping secrets, and apparently this is one of them."

"It's not exactly a secret, but there are all kinds of ways to make that happen," he said with a mysterious air.

Jess gave him a side-eye as she created a label for the bottle. "Fine. You know more, but I'm obviously not ready to hear it." When Maestro didn't care to discuss something, Jess was learning to be patient, which wasn't easy for her. Besides, she would simply ask her mother again—whenever she decided to grace them with her witchy ghost presence.

That was another thing. How could her mom only appear at the cottage and still know everything that was going on in town?

"Isn't Officer Fine stopping by this morning?" the cat said, casually dropping the reminder.

The swish of his fluffy tail told her how much he relished flustering her. Also, she suspected it was a ruse to move her train of thought along. The sooner she managed to train her mind not to let him tap into her thoughts and feelings, the happier she would be.

She glanced up at the clock. "Darn. He's probably here already. Before she realized she was doing it, a hand went up to smooth her auburn hair, which had grown well past her shoulders. She caught a knowing glance from Maestro. "Stop that."

He chuckled and waited for her to open the window to let him out. Animals were not permitted in the kitchen, but Maestro was more than a cat. As her familiar, he was in charge of her training wheels and had a great deal of knowledge of her talent in potions. Therefore he was an exception—in every way.

He turned just before he jumped outside and winked. "Yes, I am."

"That's not exactly what I thought, and I told you to stop reading my mind," she scolded.

"Then hurry up and learn to control it."

She sighed. "I've tried, but just when I think I've got the hang of blocking you out, you pop in my head like an annoying fly."

"Charming. Try harder."

Jess poked out her tongue and closed the window, narrowly missing his tail. She'd bet he was the bossiest familiar alive. That made her chuckle. A few short months ago she would have laughed in the face of anyone who told her she was a witch or that witches were real. It still bothered her that she hadn't figured out that her mother was one.

In the store, Officer Fine was leaning on the counter chatting to Jenny. He certainly was fine. Tall and dark-haired, he often kept a serious manner, but when he smiled he was downright handsome. "Sorry to keep you waiting, Officer." He'd told her to call him Brodie, but it didn't seem right when he was in uniform.

He turned and smiled broadly, causing her heart to flutter. Darn that smile.

"No problem. Do you have time to go for coffee? It's a lovely morning."

"Is this business or pleasure?" She immediately regretted her comment when he raised an eyebrow and her cheeks pinked. It had been years since she had felt attracted to a man this way or thought one was interested in her.

"Well, I know we both find a decent cup of coffee pleasurable, but there is something I'd like to discuss."

"In that case, coffee it is." She retrieved her bag, trying not to look too delighted about spending time with him.

"Have fun, you two." Jenny grinned and waved.

Her assistant was already ensconced in the store and in the apartment above it when Jess came home for her mother's funeral. It was part of the conditions of her inheritance that Jess kept Jenny employed and let her stay in the apartment. It still irked her that Mom used blackmail to persuade Jess into staying in Good Fortune—but not as much as it had. Slowly, she had begun to fit into the world she'd run away from twenty years ago.

Her midlife woes of loneliness and working at a job she hated were suddenly swept aside by her mother's death. Thrust into her new life as a trainee witch, shop owner, and employer, the only thing that had remained the same were the annoying hot flashes. She was only forty-five, and until the cat mentioned this was her midlife and a normal age for witches to gain their power, she hadn't considered she was anywhere near middle-aged.

According to Maestro, hot flashes should be welcomed as they heralded her powers gaining strength. Of course he was not only a cat but was also a male cat. Therefore, he had no concept of how debilitating a hot flash could be—and certainly no empathy.

They walked the few yards to the diner, and she chose a table away from the front window. From experience, Jess knew that Officer Fine got a lot of attention, which could be annoying when she wanted to chat in private. She had to admit to being curious.

"What's up?" she asked him casually after he'd ordered their drinks. She liked that he remembered what she drank. No other man she dated ever had. Not that there were many of those—men or dates.

He clasped his hands together on the tabletop. "I just wanted to give you a heads up that we've closed the case."

"On my mother?" she asked carefully.

He looked nonplussed. "Your mother? I meant Gerald Urwin."

She blinked. Of course he meant Gerald. The next-door neighbor was found buried in her mother's garden after Lissa died, and the how of it had never been uncovered.

"Sorry, I was confused because you never found out how he got into the garden. So how can the case be closed?"

He twirled the salt shaker, which sprayed white granules over the crisp white table cloth and absently brushed them onto the floor. "That is true. With no tire tracks and no evidence of another person being nearby, for the first time in my career I'm truly lost how or why he was buried there."

The why was easier—an aneurism, the coroner said. Jess knew that wasn't entirely the truth, but it meant that technically there was no murderer running loose. Having no idea that Gerald had in fact killed her mother with a slow and apparently undetectable poison, the police understandably had other things to deal with.

"I guess sometimes a case never gets solved, and you can hardly blame yourself when you've been so thorough." Unfortunately, Jess couldn't tell him the truth without exposing her witchy beginnings. Not then and not now.

Rubbing his fingers through his hair, he sighed. "Thanks for the pep talk. I know you're right, but you have no idea how frustrating it is. Plus, my boss likes to throw it in my face every now and again. It's ruining any chance of a promotion."

Jess's heart sank. Now she started to feel responsible for

Brodie's dilemma? It was too much, and she looked away from his despair.

A young man sat to her left. He had the local paper open on his table but was watching them. She had seen him a few times around town with another man, and he had always smiled in a friendly way. Now he looked troubled.

Suddenly she had an urge to talk to her mother that was too strong to ignore. Jess cut short the coffee break, thankful that Brodie had ordered takeout cups.

"Thanks so much for letting me know about the case being closed. I better get back and do some work, and don't let your boss's attitude get you down. You're good at your job, and he can't but help notice that."

Smiling, he stood and saw her out, his hand on the small of her back. She fancied that he was disappointed the coffee break was over, and she couldn't help being pleased.

"Excuse me, Officer?"

They turned to find the young man behind them.

"I'm sorry to intrude, but could we talk?"

"Is it a private matter, sir?"

"Well..." The man shook his head firmly. "My father didn't return home last night, and I'm worried about him."

"Is he in ill health?"

"Not that I know of."

"I'll leave you to it, Brodie," Jess said, sorry for the man who did look upset.

Chapter Two

Jess hurried right by her store and continued home. Luckily the cottage was at the other end of Main Street from the diner.

Lissa Lavender appeared as soon as the cottage door was shut. "You look a little upset, darling girl."

"I've just been talking to the police. They've closed the case on Gerald Urwin. What do you think about that?"

Her mother's ghostly body flickered a little, and she pursed her lips. "We should probably move on from that and concentrate on who we can help."

The hot, clammy hand of a hot flash crept over Jess. It seemed to happen more regularly these days and even more so when she was stressed. The funny thing was she hadn't felt overly stressed until that meeting.

"Don't you care that someone buried him in your garden?"

"Since I'm already dead, none of that sorry business can hurt me now."

This was an outright lie, so obvious it made the flickering get worse.

"Look, I get that you feel guilty about Gerald's death, but he died from an aneurism that could have killed him anytime."

"It wasn't anytime. It was after an argument with me."

"You have to let that go, Mom. Concentrate instead on the fact that the body in the garden could tarnish the family reputation and therefore your store's reputation."

Her mother laughed softly. "I doubt that. Perhaps a handful of people might consider it unsavory, but most of the town won't give it a thought. Besides, it's your store now."

"Hmm." Not wanting to upset her mom further, she didn't bring up Brodie's issues.

"Goodness, you are in a mood. I have just the thing for that." Lissa floated down the hall and into the kitchen. "Take a look in the cupboard above the counter."

Jess did so and found a wicker basket filled with potion bottles she had never seen before.

"There, that pink one. Take a tablespoon of that three times a day and you'll feel like a new woman."

"Shouldn't we be able to make something to stop hot flashes all together."

Lissa tutted. "That's not a good idea. This is a light potion to elevate your positivity. Anything more will interfere with your transition from mere woman to witch."

Jess wasn't sure if she was offended by the "mere woman" thing or excited at being something more than a middle-aged woman. "About that. Why is it that witches come into their powers at midlife?"

"This is when you are mature enough to cope with the responsibility and strong enough to learn how to harness your powers."

Trusting her mother, Jess swallowed a spoonful of the liquid and immediately felt better. "I guess some people could abuse their powers."

"Unfortunately, they do. It is a very sad situation when that happens. Their familiar must step in and remove their powers—for good, if it's warranted."

Maestro was curled up on a rug by the sink, and he shuddered. "It is not pleasant for either party."

Jess recalled him saying that if she died, he died. He was older than she could contemplate and had many Lavender women to train, but she had no children, which meant the line died with her. The weight of another responsibility hit her and made her skin heat again. She tried to focus on their conversation instead of what was expected of her.

"If potions are my thing, what other kinds of witches are there?"

Her mother floated to the back door. "There are seers and elemental witches."

"Elemental?"

"Earth, wind, and fire. Come, let's go down to the shed and you can try creating a few potion spells."

"You mean different to the ones we sell in the shop?"

Her mother shrugged. "Those are harmless but helpful. Anyone with a knowledge of botany could produce them. Obviously, without a witchy hand in making them they wouldn't be as quick or as potent."

Jess laughed. "Obviously." Witches used a cauldron, which heated instantly, and with a wand the spells perfected in seconds.

Her mother dissolved, but she felt her presence as they went to the shed. Inside it was clean and tidier than any normal shed in a backyard should be. After the door was shut, Jess pulled out the cauldron from the back of the counter. It resembled a plant pot so no one would ever guess what it was, which was a good thing when her mother had so many nosey friends.

Maestro jumped up on the counter, and her mostly visible mother moved around the shed with a sigh.

"It must be hard not being able to touch anything."

"You have no idea." Lissa sighed so deep it hurt to hear it. "This place and the kitchen at the store were my life."

"And it will be again once time passes and you can try again to come back," Jess reminded her, accepting that she had never come first and that it was finally okay. Mostly.

Maestro's snort was expected and easily ignored.

Lissa smiled. "You're right. I need to stop feeling sorry for myself."

"You have every reason to be sad about dying. I'm so sorry I failed you." Jess didn't have enough power yet to bring her mom back in the moment when it was possible, despite Lissa leaving a spell for her to make. Now they had to wait a year to try again.

"There's no need to keep apologizing, dear. Things happen for a reason, and maybe me being here with you in this way is all part of the plan."

"Whose plan? Certainly not mine."

Maestro snorted again. "You might night not have chosen this life, but don't deny that you're loving not having to work at that bakery in the city."

"What's the point of denying anything when you keep reading my mind?"

He smirked. "Poor you. Besides, you're even enjoying being one of Lavender's Ladies."

"Who?"

"Lissa's friends," he said as if she were a simpleton.

"'Enjoying' might be a bit strong. Let's just say that they are growing on me—small doses are best."

"And you like making potions," he pressed.

"That is odd when growing up I hated all that stuff."

"Not so odd," her mother mused. "When you think about it, concocting potions is not so different than baking."

Jess sniffed. "It takes a lot longer to make the perfect pastry and bake it to perfection without a magic cauldron and a wand."

"Ah, but the quest for perfection is the same and not just for the taste. Am I right?"

"Sure, but no one ever died from eating a pie."

"I wouldn't be too sure about that," Lissa chuckled. "Anyway, lots of people feel better after eating pie."

Jess considered the truth of that. While she wasn't given any credit when working at the patriarchal bakery in

Portland, she heard the comments from customers and saw their faces when she loaded up the trays in the store with things she had baked. Orders steadily increased for anything she made, and customers expressed their disappointment if they were sold out.

"Exactly." Maestro nodded.

She glared at him, wishing the power to block him would come yesterday. It was getting more annoying and embarrassing to think how much of her life he had been privy to over the last five years since her mom gave the cat to her on her fortieth birthday. Little did she know back then what was to come from such an odd choice of gift.

"I'm not the odd one."

"Enough, Maestro," Lissa admonished. "Leave Jess alone while she's studying."

He huffed and curled into a ball.

"Don't mind him. He's been bored silly for the last five years waiting for your powers to show themselves."

"He behaves like a moody teenager crossed with your worst nightmare of a teacher multiplied by a thousand."

Lissa laughed. "That is true, but he is loyal to a fault and the best teacher in the world."

"The whole world?"

Her mother winked. "The witchy world. Now, concentrate. The first potion you need to learn is one to make people forget." She winked again. "It's a spell for a short amount of time, and used right it could get you out of sticky situations."

"What kind of sticky situations?"

Lissa sighed. "There are so many I wouldn't know where to begin. Say you were caught casting a spell. You could slip the person a little sip, and they would forget what they saw in that moment only."

"Hmm. How exactly do you slip someone a potion?"

"That is something else again. A witch must be inventive in and out of the kitchen." Lissa pointed to the cauldron. "You know how to start things off."

Jess looked into the pot and waited for the glimmer of light in the bottom to turn into a mist and deliver her wand. She had yet to figure out how it got from the cauldron at the store kitchen to here. According to her mom, every witch had their own base of spells that they could use in any cauldron, and now she could test that out.

Once the cauldron activated and she held the wand, it was a matter of throwing in herbs and other odd ingredients as per her mother's instructions. Unlike baking, there was little in the way of measuring. A pinch here and a handful there. She found that if she focused on how much her mother took it would work out right. Luckily, they had the same-sized hands.

When the potion was done, she filled a small bottle with the ingredients and watched with admiration as the pot self-cleaned. She hated house work and loved this aspect of potion making.

"Jessica? Yoo-hoo! Are you out here?"

"Mrs. Crandle!" the three of them whispered.

NEED TO KEEP READING?

Get your copy of Witchy Hot Spells today!

And why not give Jessica Lavender's recipe for Cherry Jelly Pies a try?

RECIPES

These recipes are ones I use all the time and have come down the generations from my mum, grandmother, and some I have adapted from other recipes.

Also, I am now in possession of my husband's grandmother's recipe book. Exciting! I'll be bringing some of them to life very soon.

Just a wee reminder that I am a New Zealander. Occasionally, I may have missed converting into ounces and pounds for my American readers.

My apologies for that, and please let me know if you do try them and how they turn out.

Keep well.
Cheryl x

CHERRY JELLY PIES

Ingredients

1 packet of sweet short pastry sheets. (4 sheets)
1 jar of cherries with juice
1 packet of cherry jelly

Instructions

1 Heat oven to 200C or 390F
2 Heat 1 cup of the cherry syrup and add the jelly. Stir until dissolved.
3 Drain cherries and chop or tear in half.
4 Wipe 2 x 12 hole patty pans with a little butter. (Even in a non-stick pan I do this.)
5 Cut out 24 circles from the pastry to fit the pan and another 24 for the lids in a smaller size. (You'll have to roll out the leftovers to make some of them.)
6 Place a tablespoon of cherries in each and 2 tsps of jelly/syrup.
7 Put on lids and press gently around edges to close.
8 Make a small cut in the top of each to allow steam to escape.

CHERRY JELLY PIES

9 Place in oven on mid to lower shelf and bake for 15 - 20 minutes until brown.

10 Sprinkle a little icing (confectioner's) sugar on the top when cool.

ALSO BY C. A. PHIPPS

Midlife Potions - Paranormal Cozy Mysteries

Witchy Awakening

Witchy Hot Spells

Witchy Flash Back

Witchy Bad Blood - coming soon!

The Maple Lane Cozy Mysteries

Sugar and Sliced - Maple Lane Prequel

Apple Pie and Arsenic

Bagels and Blackmail

Cookies and Chaos

Doughnuts and Disaster

Eclairs and Extortion

Fudge and Frenemies

Gingerbread and Gunshots

Honey Cake and Homicide - preorder now!

Beagle Diner Cozy Mysteries

Beagles Love Cupcake Crimes

Beagles Love Steak Secrets

Beagles Love Muffin But Murder

Beagles Love Layer Cake Lies

The Cozy Café Mysteries

Sweet Saboteur

Candy Corruption

Mocha Mayhem

Berry Betrayal

Deadly Desserts

Please note: Most are also available in paperback and some in audio.

Remember to join Cheryl's Cozy Mystery newsletter.
There's a free recipe book waiting for you.
Cheryl also writes romance as Cheryl Phipps.

ABOUT THE AUTHOR

'Life is a mystery. Let's follow the clues together.'

C. A. Phipps is a USA Today best-selling author from beautiful New Zealand. Cheryl is an empty-nester living in a quiet suburb with her wonderful husband, 'himself'. With an extended family to keep her busy when she's not writing, there is just enough space for a crazy mixed breed dog who stole her heart! She enjoys family times, baking, and her quest for the perfect latte.

Check out her website http://caphipps.com

- facebook.com/authorcaphipps
- x.com/CherylAPhipps
- instagram.com/caphippsauthor

Made in United States
North Haven, CT
09 June 2024

53414336R00104